ISBN: 9798651446780

IMPRINT: Independently published.

Cover design by Nicole Carter

FOR MY FAMILY

EIGHTEEN YEARS AGO
HAZEL

"Hold her steady!"

I listened and watched as their army used their pitiful abilities against me. They didn't stand a chance.

I had one fool holding one of my wrists, and another fool holding the other. The stench was overwhelming. A flick of my wrist and they'd be gone.

The lot of them.

"Get ready men!"

Their pathetic leader shouted his orders, standing like a coward in the crops of trees.

I would put up with their antics for only a moment longer.

I started with the fool barking orders. He didn't see it coming; the moment I wrapped an invisible pair of hands around his throat. I could hear his windpipe squeezing shut even from this distance.

His gasps of air came next as he frantically clawed at his throat for a reprieve. It didn't take long for him to fall to his knees, his body spent.

It was at this time that his cronies faltered, and it was enough for me to gain the upper hand. As their grip lessened, my abilities released to their entirety. My wrists turned into hot coals beneath their palms, burning them intensely.

They fell to the ground.

I held my palms near their hearts, waiting for the delectable energy to seep into my senses. I breathed in deep as their souls flowed into me.

I opened my eyes and looked across the clearing. It only took my gaze for the rest of them to turn and run.

CHAPTER ONE
WILLOW

An explosion of bright, purple light lit up the thicket of trees that surrounded me. It was an eerie brightness that only lasted for a few seconds, but it was long enough to see the dozens of ruby-red eyes staring back at me.

I turned to run and stumbled over a jagged tree branch that had fallen to the ground. I fell and hit the earth hard enough to rattle my teeth. My heart was pounding and although my hands were shaking I managed to brace them on the leaf-covered floor to push myself to a standing position. As I straightened my leg a searing hot pain erupted along the length of it and I had to bite my lip to stop myself from screaming.

I tried to assess the damage and winced as I found a sharp branch embedded in my flesh. It had pierced straight through my thigh. The pointed end was covered in warm, sticky blood and the metallic odour was overwhelming. I whimpered as it sent another twinge of pain down my leg.

Furiously, I wiped the tears from my face and looked around. It took a while for my eyes to adjust to the darkness but it was clear I was at the border. I hadn't realised how far I had run. I was so far from home.

I looked around to determine which way to go and began to walk as best as I could with my leg dragging behind me as I moved towards Ignis. The blood was beginning to gush from the wound no matter how much pressure I was applying and the point of the branch was digging into the palm of my hand.

It didn't matter how quietly I tried to move, the sound of crunching leaves was so loud that I couldn't hide if I tried, and despite how well I knew the forest, navigating through the waist-high thickets and weeds with a lame leg was no easy task.

The further I walked away from the border the crunchier the leaves, and the snapping of fallen twigs was more frequent. I knew without seeing that the leaves were becoming more autumnal and the reds and oranges were vivid in my mind.

The trees were becoming thicker, and I could feel myself relax knowing that I was almost home despite the excruciating pain that was shooting down my leg with every step that I took.

Suddenly, the ground erupted into flames around me. The red-hot fire was almost as tall as me and the flames trapped me in every direction. I tried to call for help but the smoke was already filling my lungs. As I coughed, I fell to my knees. I was surrounded by thick, grey smoke and my throat felt as if it, too, was on fire. Whenever I tried to take a breath, my throat stung from the ashes and my heart pounded in my chest; the sound seeming so loud as if it was reverberating around me.

"Willow!" I jumped at the sound of my name. My brother's voice echoed around me and my eyes snapped open. My heart still pounded inside my chest but I felt myself relax when I realised I was home.

My brother's eyes were wide and his skin had paled from his usual tan. He was pacing on the spot unable to do anything about the flames that were still surrounding me. I caught the look of utter panic on his face and sat up in bed.

I waved my right hand dismissing the flames which left behind a black, dense fog and the smell of burning fabric, despite there not being a shred of damage.

"Are you okay?" Aspen sat on the edge of my bed and pulled me into a hug. It took a moment to get over the surprise of his rare affection.

I pulled out of his embrace and leaned back against the headboard. I tried not to wince as the pain shot down my leg again. He didn't know yet how real the dreams were. "Aspen, I'm fine. Really. Don't stress. It happens all the time."

"How can I not stress? One day you are not going to wake up in time. Seriously, you need to see somebody about this."

"Will you calm down, please?"

"As soon as dad wakes up I'll have a word with him. He must know a way to help."

I looked at my brother. He had always been a worrier where I had always been the carefree one. The colour was slowly returning to his face, a soft brown from hours outside in the training ring. It only accentuated the bright green of his eyes.

It reminded me of how different we both were and looked. Aspen had inherited our father's green eyes and brown curls. I had the long, wavy brown hair of my mother, but neither of my parents had the same blue eyes.

"Aspen, my birthday is in two weeks and then I can start to control it. You remember what it was like, don't you? There isn't much you can do until you Awaken."

Aspen turned to face me. "I know all that, but I didn't wake up every night nearly burning myself alive."

I sighed. "It will get better. You'll see."

I rose from the bed and went over to the window. The pain in my thigh had eased considerably now there was no branch poking through it. It would soon heal; they always did.

The sun was beginning to rise and with the warm orange glow I could just make out the ripple between this world and the human realm beyond. I had always wondered what it had been like before Sationem had been created. It was said that the humans feared magic and so the four founders created our world so we could live peacefully.

Aspen's voice tore me from my thoughts. "Willow, I just need you to be careful, okay? This isn't normal." I agreed with him, although I would never admit it.

"Why don't you go and lie down?" I said. There were dark circles around his eyes. He looked exhausted. "I'm going to go for a walk."

I noticed his tense shoulders relax and I knew that he was relieved that I wasn't going back to sleep. I watched as his got up and left the room, glancing back at me before entering his own, and I felt myself become teary; my brother's stress and tiredness was my fault.

CHAPTER TWO
WILLOW

A carpet of red, yellow and orange crunched underfoot as I made my way over to the campfire of the community ground.

I collapsed into the wicker chair I had left there the evening before. I listened intently to the early morning sounds, birds singing in the distance and insects chirping, and closed my eyes. I couldn't get the dream out of my head. The fire didn't scare me at all, but the red eyes and the creatures they belonged to were terrifying.

The Superno were terrifying creatures, the Shadows especially. Their aim was simple: to kill.

I took a deep breath, trying to block them from my mind, but it was the darkness that they liked anyway. Dad had always told us stories about them. He explained that they had originated from the human realm when Sationem was created. They could barely survive in a world where our gifts were so widely used, so they had adapted to their new climate when the new atmosphere engulfed them.

The Superno divided.

The Auroras took to the new world well, they were almost identical to the Shadow Superno except for their colouring and protected whoever entered the forest.

The Shadows were not so lucky. They didn't cope well with the change and something happened to make them fear others.

I awoke to the warm sun on my face. It had fully risen now so I must have fallen asleep. I lifted myself further into the chair, grimacing at the pain in my neck. I must have been asleep in a weird position.

"Hey, Willow."

"Hi Olive."

She sat on the grass next to me. "How long have you been out here?" she asked.

I shrugged my shoulders. "I have no idea. A few hours, I think."

We sat in silence for a while. Olive was looking down at the ground playing with a blade of grass. She was small for her short years. Blonde hair fell in waves down her back, falling over and hiding her face. Hours spent in the sun brought out the freckles that covered almost every inch of her skin.

"What's wrong?" I asked, playfully nudging Olives shoulder. She murmured something that I couldn't quite hear.

"Olive speak up honey. I can't hear you." She looked up then, her blue eyes bright against the sunlight.

"It's nothing."

"It must be something." I slid out of the chair to sit cross-legged in front of the young girl.

"It's just that my brother has started showing signs of his abilities, and however hard I try, nothing happens." Her voice started to break and her eyes were brimming with tears.

"Honey, come here, come here," I pulled her into a hug. "Olive, listen to me okay? Linden is three years older than you, which is the normal time for his abilities to be showing. I know it's not what you want to hear, but it's just a waiting game. It's going to be another couple of years yet before you notice anything happening."

"It's so far away though," she said, sniffling.

"Olive, you're ten years old. You need to enjoy being a kid while you still can."

"That's easy for you to say. You'll be eighteen soon and then you can do whatever you want."

I sighed. "Growing up is harder than you think."

"You're just saying that," she said. I raised my eyebrows and Olive shrugged. "Thanks for listening anyway."

"No problem." We both got to our feet. Olive smiled at me and ran home.

Aspen was at the kitchen table when I got back inside. The house was quieter than usual.

"Wheres's mom?" I asked.

Aspen took a bite of his apple and shrugged. "I have no idea."

I frowned. Mom was always up before any of us. I walked down the narrow hallway and knocked softly on their bedroom door. There was no answer so I pushed the door open a crack.

"They aren't here," I said as I walked back into the kitchen.

"They probably had an early morning meeting or something," Aspen said as he finished off his breakfast. "Don't worry about it."

He was probably right so I sat down and helped myself to some fruit.

***

The rest of the day passed in a blur, I didn't do much other than lounge around outside listening to and watching the Youngers as they practised their abilities and catching up on some much-needed sleep.

My parents didn't come home, and we had heard no word from them.

CHAPTER THREE
WILLOW

I had had a restless night but thankfully without any fire. I had tossed and turned thinking about my parents. I knew Aspen hadn't slept either as his bedroom light had been on for most of the night.

I couldn't remember a day going by when I hadn't seen my mom. Her long brown hair would seem to shimmer in the light matching the colour of her eyes. Her friendly face in the morning was something that I looked forward to.

My dad quite often spent nights away from home for work as he was responsible for making sure that each Zone had the fuel and heat that it needed. He was always a fire message away though.

I couldn't send fire messages until I Awakened, but Aspen could.

I jumped out of bed and ran for the door.

My brother was pacing back and forth in the kitchen until he noticed me and sat down at the table.

"Aspen, have you sent dad a fire message?" I asked breathlessly. I don't know why I hadn't thought of it before.

"Of course. I haven't had a reply yet."

I sighed and sat down opposite my brother.

"I've called a meeting at Crownfire." Aspen held his head in his hands. He was stressed which made him seem older, despite his twenty-three years.

"Do you think it's come to that?" Calling a meeting was not something that you did lightly.

"I don't know, Willow. Something doesn't feel right and I can't sit around doing nothing."

"What time is the meeting?"

"Midday."

***

The closer we walked to the centre, the thinner the trees became. Neutral ground was always open to the elements and was a place where all Zones could meet peacefully. It was where trading could take place and where the Tree Leaders held their meetings.

Aspen was up ahead; he was walking a lot faster and I could tell he was nervous. He never had been very comfortable at gatherings and the Tree Leaders were certainly intimidating.

I ran to catch up with him but tripped over a rock jutting out from the ground. I stumbled to the ground, unable to save myself, and braced for the impact. It didn't come.

I opened eyes, not having realised that I had shut them, and saw that I was hovering just a few inches from the ground.

This wasn't good. I started to panic and then I felt the world tip beneath me and I fell with a loud thump. I scrambled to stand and hastily brushed the dirt off my clothes.

"Willow?" My eyes widened as I heard my brother's voice I hoped he hadn't seen.

"Yeah?' I walked quickly towards his voice.

"What's taking you so long? The meeting starts soon."

I veered left and found Aspen waiting for me. I could see his hands shaking and I knew that I couldn't speak to him yet of what had happened. Not yet.

I couldn't have an ability that belonged to another Zone. It shouldn't be possible. I had heard about an ability called wind generation that could create blasts of air. Maybe that's what I had done?

We were close to the centre now and I could sense the magic that surrounded this area of the forest. Crownfire was just up ahead and the Tree Leaders were already in position. They stared down at us from high up on their platforms.

As we neared the clearing I was careful to watch out for the flames. They were almost invisible and surrounded the entire meeting area. You could only see them if you were *really* looking, but even then, it was more like flickers that you could out of the corner of your eye.

"Willow," Aspen's whispered voice brought me back to the present. He took my hand and led me to the empty platform on our right. I kept my eyes on the ground as we took the position that our parents usually did.

I braced myself as the platform lifted us up and over the flames and into the centre of Crownfire, and face-to-face with the other Tree Leaders.

"Welcome, children. What can we do for you?" I looked up as Lily, the Second Leader from Terra spoke to us. Her hair was long and golden, curling down almost to her waist. Her eyes shone a bright green against the flames. "Where are your parents?"

"We were hoping you could tell us?" Aspen said.

"Why would you ask that?"

Aspen was about to answer when I cut in instead. "Well, they are Tree Leaders and so are you. Did you send them somewhere or ask them to do something?"

The other Tree Leaders looked at each other. There was silence for a while.

"Unfortunately, we do not have the power to order each other around, child, as much as we would like to." Oakley spat out. He was the Second Leader from Glacies. His white hair and beard clearly showed that he was the eldest Leader. His cold, black pinprick eyes seemed to pierce right into your mind. As he spoke the fire turned black around us.

"Calm down Oakley," Lily said. "We're all on the same side here." The fire glowed yellow around Lily when she spoke.

I remembered being told about the fire surrounding Crownfire by my parents. The flames changed colour when each of the Leaders spoke. The colour of the fire changed depending on their moods. When a meeting was in session the flames are green. The flames will then turn blue if they're upset, dark red if they're angry, yellow if they're happy. Also, if one is thinking particularly evil thoughts, then the fire will turn black.

The reason for this is so the Tree Leaders can get an inkling of the others' thoughts and feelings. They can know when someone is lying as the fire will send up shoots of red sparks when this happens.

"I am sure they will turn up soon." This time it was Blue who spoke. His voice was quiet but firm. He was the First Leader from

Ventus. His blue eyes big and bright, and his hair as black as the night. "If Cedar and Maple are not back by the full moon, then please let us know."

We both nodded as we were dismissed from the meeting. There was no use in arguing. The full moon was in a week. They would be back.

As the platforms landed on each side of the Centre, I watched intriguingly as the Tree Leaders used their abilities to get home.

Blue and his sister, Poppy from Ventus disappeared inside a tornado using Aeroportation; their black hair standing out through the wind. Dune and his wife, Lily from Terra disappeared into the ground like moles using Terraportation. Oakley and his wife, Crimson from Glacies disappeared in a rush of water using Hydroportation. Our parents could teleport too, through fire. Pyroportation.

Aspen was watching them too, a look between admiration and anger on his face. I could tell that he wasn't happy about how the Tree Leaders dismissed us so easily. They didn't seem to be as concerned as we were.

***

When I finally settled down in bed that night my mind kept wandering over the day's events, in particular the ability I had shown in the forest. I was secretly pleased that I was different than the rest of my family, but I knew they would never understand. I had never heard of anyone in Ignis having abilities other than fire.

One thing was certain.

I couldn't tell anyone.

CHAPTER FOUR
WILLOW

I hadn't slept well at all. I tossed and turned in-between the hot flushes. My dreams consisted of hovering high up in the sky and falling at an alarming rate back to the ground where I would wake again in a hot sweat. Each time I could feel my heart thumping inside my chest. I felt for sure that it was going to beat right out of my body.

The dreams freaked me out, but what scared me the most was that I didn't know what I was doing in the real world. If I dreamed of fire when it surrounded me in bed, then was I hovering in bed too? I didn't want Aspen to find me like that.

I walked into the kitchen to find my brother already up and dressed. He was usually the last one up; I rarely saw him before midday. Although he didn't look tired, his hair was stuck up all over the place as if he had just rolled out of bed.

"Did you sleep well?" I asked.

"Better than I thought," he shrugged.

I relaxed slightly, the tension in my shoulders easing. There was nothing in Aspen's tone to suggest that he had seen anything untoward during the night.

"What's the plan today?"

"What makes you think I have a plan?" Aspen asked. I gave him a sceptical look and raised my eyebrows. He laughed. "Okay, okay, I do. We are going to go and look through mom and dad's room, see if there's anything to suggest where they might be."

I poured myself a bowl of cereal and sat at the table. "Do you think there will be anything?"

"I don't know," he said, shrugging his shoulders. "We have to do something though and it's the only place I can think of looking right now."

I nodded. It sounded as good an idea as any.

***

We were supposed to ask permission to enter our parents' room so standing at the door and crossing the threshold seemed like an impossible task. I found myself rooted to the spot, despite my brother waltzing straight in.

The bedroom was so tidy that the bed looked as if it had never been slept in. The crisp white covers were clean and straight, and the dark wooden matching dresser, drawers and wardrobe all seemed normal other than a slight covering of dust.

"Willow, what's wrong? Come on." I dropped my hand from which I had inadvertently been chewing at my fingernails and followed him into the room, one step at a time. My feet sank into the thick beige carpet and, although I felt guilty, I knew that it had to be done.

I didn't know where to start so I sat down in front of the old wooden trunk at the foot of the bed. I pulled at the clasp to open it upwards and it creaked as I slowly lifted the heavy lid.

"Hey look, it's all our old baby stuff," I said, pulling out a tiny blue baby outfit. Aspen looked over and took it from me.

"Wow, it's so tiny," he said, holding out the little arms and legs of the suit.

"I know, they're adorable," I said as I pulled out another outfit with matching shoes. This one was a yellow dress with little frills all over it. It was mine.

"Just remember we are looking for the whereabouts of mom and dad, not reminiscing."

"I know."

Aspen went back over to the drawers on the far side of the room to continue looking through its contents whilst I continued rummaging through the bottom of the trunk. There were some photographs right at the bottom. I pulled them out and sat back on my heels. They were all of Aspen as a baby and a few when he was older too.

When I was eight, I had asked my parents why there weren't any photos of me around the house. They said there had been a fire and that all the photographs had been burnt. Even then, I had thought that my parents were lying; they lived in a community where everyone over the age of eighteen could control fire and, yet no one could save the photographs.

I dug around the bottom of the trunk to make sure I had gotten everything only I could feel a ridge in the wood, but more pronounced. I carefully and slowly lifted the loose wood disguised as the base of the trunk. There were more photographs underneath.

I lifted them out to see that the photographs were of myself when I was a baby, a little older when I was around five-years and some a little older than that. My parents had lied to me.

There was a common strangeness to each photo in that I had a golden glow around my entire body. I thought I was imagining it but it was too clear.

"Have you found anything yet?" Aspen asked, making me jump.

Hastily I threw the photographs back into the bottom of the trunk. "Not yet, what about you?"

Aspen sighed. "Nothing," he shrugged his shoulders, clearly deflated. I knew how hopeful he had been. "Maybe we should take a break and have some lunch."

I nodded and Aspen left the room. I threw everything back into the trunk, all except for one picture of myself which I slipped into my pocket.

I joined Aspen in the kitchen, the sweet aroma of liquorice root tea was inviting and I sat down at the table after he handed me a cup. I breathed it in and I instantly felt myself relax.

A strange pounding underneath my feet had me looking up at Aspen who had felt it too.

"What is that?" I asked.

The pounding became more intense making my ears ring. Aspen ran outside and I followed closely behind. We weren't the only ones; our immediate community had gathered to see what was happening.

Everybody was looking around trying to find the source of the disturbance. It seemed to have eased slightly as the ringing in my ears had dulled.

I heard a distant scream and then I saw it. A small revolving tornado appeared from around a bend. A few people almost flew back to their houses but my feet were rooted to the spot. I had never seen anything like it. It travelled closer until it came to a stop before Aspen and me.

The gale it blew was strong and after spinning a few more times disappeared altogether. I was now looking into the bright eyes of Blue, the Tree Leader from Ventus.

It seemed to take him a minute to get his bearings, but when he did, he smiled.

It was rare for anyone to enter a Zone that they didn't belong to so I wasn't the only one who looked shocked. Nobody said a word as Blue looked around and took in the surroundings. Anyone other than a Tree Leader would need permission to enter and it suddenly dawned on me that the pounding was a warning that Blue had entered Ignis without permission.

"Blue," Aspen said, raising his eyebrows. "What can we do for you?"

"I apologise for coming by unannounced," he said. "I wish to speak with you and your sister if that's alright?" he looked from Aspen to me for an answer.

"Of course," Aspen replied. "Please come in and sit down." He gestured to the house and Blue and I followed him inside.

My brother and I sat on one side of the table and Blue the other. I looked at him curiously.

"What was it you wanted to talk to us about?" Aspen asked.

"Your parents," Blue said. "I wanted to see if you've had any contact?"

Aspen shook his head. "Nothing. It's so out of character for them. Have you heard anything? Do you know what's happened?"

"I'm sorry but I don't. I am going to speak to the other Tree Leaders. Could you meet us at Crownfire tomorrow? At midday? We have a lot to discuss."

"That's it? You don't have any information that you can tell us now?"

"I'm afraid not."

"But you have some information?"

"Not about your parents, no. I cannot discuss anything else here. We will speak tomorrow." Blue got up out of his seat and crossed over to the door. "I'll see you tomorrow," he smiled.

I couldn't keep my eyes off him. There was a lightness about him that made him seem to glide across the floor.

I was desperate to see him use his abilities again. I was fascinated by the mechanics of teleportation and I felt my eyes widen as the tornado formed in front of me. It was like a dense fog that seemed to swallow him up and a strong breeze was left in his wake.

I went back inside to my brother leaving the residents of our community gossiping about this behind me. This has probably been the most exciting thing to happen in years.

Aspen wasn't in a good way when I reached the kitchen. He's in a bad mood, I could tell straight away that he was frustrated. His face was scrunched up in a frown and he was slamming things around.

"Aspen, you need to calm down," I said cautiously. It was inevitable what was about to happen.

"Don't tell me what to do Willow!" he shouted. His words were streaked with anger and I sighed and stepped backwards.

A fire erupted behind him and the white-hot flames towered above him. Pyrokinesis was useful and the most used ability in Ignis but it was tainted by emotions. Aspen had conjured the fire, willingly or not, and he was the only one who could control it.

"Aspen!" I waved my arms around trying desperately to get his attention and to pull him back. I tried to use my abilities as rare as it was that I'd be able to extinguish the flames myself. Nothing.

At the sound of my voice, Aspen shuddered a little which seemed to bring him back to his senses. The flames disappeared leaving behind a smoky hue and Aspen collapsed on a chair at the kitchen table.

"I'm sorry. I'm not angry at you, I'm angry at him," he said nodding towards the door.

"Blue?"

"Of course. Who else? What was the point of him coming here? He didn't tell us anything that we didn't already know. He just got our hopes up." Aspen said bitterly.

"He was being nice, that's all."

"Why are you defending him?" Aspen questioned.

"I'm not. I just thought it was a kind gesture. He cares, otherwise, why did he come?"

Aspen banged his fist on the table. It reverberated across the wood making me jump. "You need to get your head out of the clouds, Willow. Tree Leaders don't do things without a reason."

"Be careful, Aspen. Mom and dad are Tree Leaders too, remember."

He didn't bother answering me. Instead, he left the room without another word and stomped down the hallway. A few seconds later his bedroom door slammed shut.

I sighed. I didn't like my brother and I fighting. It didn't happen often which meant that the fights were usually worse than simple bickering.

I pulled the photograph from my pocket. I couldn't make any sense of it and I didn't want Aspen seeing it. Not yet.

CHAPTER FIVE
WILLOW

I was sitting on an old rickety chair in the front garden. The sun had just risen, warming my face and casting a golden glow over Ignis. The sky was blue with not a cloud in sight. A perfect day and yet my stomach was in knots. It wouldn't be long until we had to leave for Crownfire.

"Willow, I need to practise my flying, " Olive had made her way over to me. Her long curly hair was pulled up today and it made her look a little older.

"Okay, honey. Just a second." I closed my eyes and concentrated.

"Thanks, Willow," Olive said happily.

I opened my eyes to see the Benu standing tall and proud in front of me. Its wings had a span of at least two metres and the edge of one red wing brushed the side of the house. The Benu was an elemental bird native to the Ignis Zone and was a great training aid. It helped the Youngers to practice their flying, and at the same time, it helped them to control their abilities.

I concentrated long enough for Olive to jump on the Benu's back, grabbing hold of its long red and orange feathers, and I watched as she managed to hover a few feet from the ground. As soon as her abilities strengthened, she would be able to fly as high as she liked.

Thick grey smoke began to rise and surround the young girl which was an indication that the magic was wearing off. Unfortunately, if the rider was young or inexperienced the magic only lasted a short while. In a way, it was convenient as I knew the Youngers would never give up their fly time otherwise.

"It's time to jump off then, Olive," I shouted. At my demand, she jumped off the bird, rolled along the ground as I'd taught her and jumped to her feet.

Immediately the Benu erupted into flames before disappearing into a pile of ash. There was a chorus of joyful clapping and whistling as the bird disappeared and Olive jumped up and down clapping her hands with the biggest grin on her face.

"Thanks, Willow." Olive ran over to hug me before running off to join her friends at the training ground.

"Well done, sweetie."

I sighed, remembering the days where I had nothing to worry about except training. I wished I could go back. There was still so much that needed to be done, especially with my Awakening nearing. I wanted to train more than anything but there was far too much to worry about. Before my parents went missing, I was in the middle of learning heliokinesis, so I could manipulate and control the sun and sunlight. It was a useful ability and not one that everybody usually achieved. I was doing well, but I hadn't practised for a long while.

"Willow, it's time to go," I turned around to see Aspen in the doorway. He was standing stiffly and his knuckles were white on the doorframe. The Tree Leaders made him uneasy and I knew that he wouldn't relax until we were on the way home.

We didn't talk on the way. Aspen was quiet, staring straight ahead. He always acted tough and confident, but I knew differently. He was a lot more sensitive than he let on.

Crownfire looked the same, although it felt like a lifetime since we had been here last. The centre was quiet except for the quiet hum of magic that I had come to recognise. The Tree Leaders were in place already.

I side-stepped the red, flickering flames that surrounded the meeting place to get to the empty platform. I took hold of the surrounding rail for support as we lurched forwards and then came to a stop with a jolt.

"Welcome," the familiar sound of Blues voice echoed around us. I looked up at my brother who nodded his head in response.

I then looked around. Blue and his sister Poppy looked the friendliest out of everyone. Poppy had long, black hair and bright, blue eyes that matched her brothers. She had a warm smile that made talking to her and being in her company more inviting.

When my eyes settled on Blue I was surprised to see that he was looking at me too. I looked down at my feet. When I looked up again, he was looking away, but he had a hint of a smile on his face.

"Could you please tell us why we are here?" Aspen asked. "Blue said that you had information?"

"What do you mean by 'Blue said' exactly?" Oaklcy's voice boomed out around us. The flames turned a deep, dark red from the loudness of his voice.

I looked over at him. Oakley lookcd so angry all the time. At thirty-five, he was the eldest of the Tree Leaders. His wife, Crimson was the first leader of Glacies. Oakley was her second. However, from the way they acted, it would be easy to think that it was the other way around. When I looked over at Crimson, she seemed to just cower behind him, her head down shyly. She never made eye contact, her long, blond hair covered most of her face, and I had never heard her speak.

"Well, Blue came to Ignis to let us know about the meeting," Aspen explained.

Almost simultaneously everybody turned to look at Blue. I looked too to see him standing with his arms crossed over his chest. He didn't seem intimidated at all.

"Explain yourself please, Blue." It was Dune that spoke this time, I hadn't heard much about him, only that he was strict but fair. All decisions that he made, he made with his wife, Lily. Most of the time, they both looked happy and laid back. Approachable.

Blue sighed. "Yes, I went to Ignis." He explained. "I wanted to see how Aspen and Willow were doing with the disappearance of their parents." He shrugged. "They had to know about the meeting anyway."

"That isn't the way to do things and you know it," Oakley said. His voice was quiet and calm and more terrifying somehow.

Blue raised his eyebrows. "It's called being considerate Oakley. Maybe you should try it sometime."

"You dare speak to me like that?" Oakley's voice was so loud that I had to cover my ears. The flames around us were glowing red one minute and black the next.

The bickering continued around Crownfire, until one by one, everyone stopped.

Suddenly, Aspen's hand was on my shoulder squeezing gently. I opened my eyes to find the flames around us glowing brightly in every colour of the rainbow.

"What the…" Oakley stuttered, and for once he seemed speechless, and then, without warning, the coloured flames were gone and everything was returned to normal.

Aspen seemed to regain his composure first. "Are you going to tell us why we are here or not?"

"We want you and Willow to take the place of your parents on the Tree Leaders Council," Dune said.

"What? They're not dead. They are missing." Aspen said angrily. "What are you doing to find them?" he asked, the flames sparking red.

"Currently, there is nothing to do until we have a clear idea of where they are, or until they make contact." Dune explained calmly.

"What if they never make contact?" Aspen asked, and my eyes widened at the question. I hadn't realised that my brother was thinking like that.

"We will deal with it then. If no contact is made within the next two weeks, we will look at other options."

"That's it?" Aspen yelled, the flames turning red once more.

"Calm down, boy!" Oakley boomed.

I felt an icy cold washing over me. Aspen must have felt it too because when he let out a breath, I could see it as a mist in front of his face. Oakley must have been using his abilities. Cryokinesis and hydrokinesis allowed him to manipulate and control ice, snow and other forms of frozen water.

"In the meantime," Dune continued. "We need you and your sister to complete the Council."

Aspen was shaking his head, and I could feel tears brimming my eyes.

"Do you both understand what is meant of you presently?" Dune asked.

I looked up at Aspen as he nodded his head. I nodded too, and as I did, I felt a light breeze blow over me. I immediately looked up to see Blue watching me. He gave me a warm smile.

"Excellent," Dune said. "We will all meet back here in two weeks. Same time."

***

"This is ridiculous," Aspen muttered, more to himself than to me as we walked home. The Tree Council had dismissed us rather abruptly after we had agreed to represent the Council. "He could have at least prepared us for that."

"Who?" I asked.

"Blue, of course." He answered sharply.

"Oh." I walked quietly for a minute. "Why can't they do anything, Aspen?" I asked, my voice breaking.

"They said that they are waiting to see if our parents make contact. They are only saying that because they don't have a clue what they are doing."

"What if they never turn up?" I asked quietly.

Aspen stopped walking and put his hands on my shoulders. "Don't worry. It's down to us now. We'll find them."

"How?"

"We know them better than anyone, right? That's got to count for something. We just need to figure out what they were doing the last time we saw them."

I nodded but I wasn't as convinced as my brother.

"Trust me, Willow."

CHAPTER SIX
WILLOW

I had been sat in the garden since our return from Crownfire. Aspen had gone inside and stayed there.

There were a few things that happened at the meeting running through my mind. The rainbow flames were baffling. I hadn't seen or heard anything like it before. I had a strange feeling that I had something to do with it. My abilities had been all over the place since the countdown to my Awakening.

I couldn't wait to control my abilities. The way Oakley had used ice during the meeting only proved that he was one of the most powerful people in Glacies. The way Blue had used his abilities to get my attention was amazing too. It wouldn't be long until I could use my abilities at will too and I couldn't wait, despite how nervous I was about it.

I had a week to go before I was eighteen and my Awakening. I knew that I wouldn't be able to control my ability straight away, but I would be able to use it freely.

I looked over at the community training ground. I could see small balls of red, orange and yellow flames being thrown around, and flickers as the smaller Youngers attempted to copy their friends and older siblings. Pyrokinesis was the first ability that Youngers were taught.

I closed my eyes and relaxed back into the chair. There was a crispness to the air which felt refreshing.

A shadow blocked the sun and I opened my eyes to see Forrest and Acacia standing in front of me. They were both fifteen-years-old and the only twins in Ignis. When they were born, it was a big deal. I was intrigued to see how their abilities worked when they Awakened. Since it is said that twins would have a deep connection with each other, my father thought that they might be able to use each other's abilities.

"Hey, guys. What's up?" I asked.

"Hi Willow," Acacia said pleasantly. "We were just wondering…"

"Wondering what?" I asked. Acacia and Forrest looked at each other, their green eyes locking together. "Guys what?"

"Well," Forrest spoke up. "We were wondering, well everyone was really, what Blue was doing here yesterday?"

"Oh that, well it was about our parents, they've been missing for a few days now and we don't have a clue where they are. He was just checking around to see if we were good." I explained.

The twins looked at each quickly, confusion on their faces.

"What is it?" I sat up in the chair.

"We saw your parents a few days ago," Acacia said.

"Where? How long ago exactly?" I said as I stood up.

The twins looked at each other for a minute. "It was late, maybe three days ago. It was well after midnight," Forrest said. "I remember because I got up for a drink of water and I saw them through the window. I thought it was a bit odd and I mentioned it to Acacia when we got up the next morning."

"Why didn't you say anything earlier?" I could feel myself starting to get irritated.

"They are our Tree Leaders, I just assumed they were off doing official business or something. I didn't know they were missing. You haven't said anything either." Forrest protested.

"You're right, sorry. I shouldn't have bitten your head off." I apologised. "Let me get Aspen so we can tell him, okay?" I left them in the garden and ran into the house.

"Aspen!" I shouted him and I didn't expect the hint of panic in my voice.

"Willow, what's wrong?" Aspen came running down the hallway from his bedroom. His eyes were wide with alarm. "What is it?"

"Come on," I said, already going back out to the garden, dragging him behind me

"Willow, will you just tell me what's going on?" Aspen said. I let go of his arm and he stopped short when he saw Acacia and Forrest waiting. "Er, hi. What's up?"

"Hi Aspen," Acacia said, shyly.

"Aspen, Forrest saw something the night mom and dad disappeared," I explained. "He saw them."

"You did?" he asked Forrest. "Where?"

"Over there," Forrest pointed towards the far edge of the forest. "They went through the trees, going North."

"What time was this?"

"I'm not sure exactly but it was late, really late. Well after midnight." Forrest answered.

Aspen grabbed my arm. "Right, come on." He started walking to where Forrest had seen them. "Thanks, guys!" he shouted over his shoulder.

I pulled my arm from his grip. "We don't even know what's out there, Aspen. Is it safe to just go wandering around?" I asked, slightly scared that my brother had seemed to have lost all sense. He never acted first, always juggling with rights and wrongs before he did anything.

"You heard him, Willow. This is the first clue we've had. Who knows if we're going to get another one. We have to at least look." He stopped and looked at me, eyes wide. Pleading.

I sighed. "Okay."

We had both walked in silence for a while before something occurred to me. "Aspen, why would they be going here, this leads to the outside border, There's nothing there."

"I don't know Willow, but they were seen walking this way, so I'm going to keep looking."

It made no sense. "What if they turned back though? Or if they started coming this way but then changed direction? What if…"

"Willow! Please, let's just see where we end up okay? Keep an eye out for anything. They might have dropped something. It might give us a clue as to where they were heading."

I let out a sigh and carried on walking. I hated it when my brother was angry. It had been a stressful few days, but I knew somehow in the back of my mind that my parents were close. They were just out of reach. I didn't know quite how to describe it.

A few minutes later, Aspen came to stop. I almost stumbled into him.

"Aspen..."

"I know."

All I could do was stare. We had never been to this area before, but everybody knew it. It had been in all the old stories.

Hazel's resting place.

CHAPTER SEVEN
WILLOW

According to the stories Hazel was a witch. An evil one at that. She had necromancy magic in her blood. It was said that she would steal the souls of people with elemental magic to make herself stronger. No one knew what happened to the people whose souls she stole.

"Aspen, you don't think…"

"No, Willow. It's impossible."

Hazel wasn't dead. Despite the area being called her resting place, she was just trapped. She was too powerful to be stopped and it took the most powerful person from each Zone to combine their abilities and trap her in a place in-between life and death: Limbus.

The disappearances stopped, however, the people whose souls she stole never returned.

"Do you feel that, Aspen?" I asked. It felt like my whole body was vibrating and a strange numbness accompanied it.

Aspen looked at me, a confused expression on his face. "Feel what?"

"Nothing," I said quickly. If this was some other ability beginning to show itself, I did not want my brother to know about it.

I walked closer to the outside border where the vibrations were more prominent. It changed to a low rumbling, like an earthquake beginning to shake. I looked over at Aspen, it was clear that he wasn't experiencing this.

"Okay, I don't think there's anything to suggest that they were here," Aspen announced. I jumped at the sound of his voice, it sounded far away, the low rumbling taking over my senses. "Let's head back home."

It took all my strength to follow my brother home. He might not have felt anything, but I knew that something was happening.

It was dark by the time we got back and the Zone was quiet.

"I'm going to bed," Aspen said as soon as we walked through the door.

"Don't you want anything to eat first?" I asked.

"I'm not hungry."

I grabbed an apple from the bowl on the table and sat down. "Where are you?" I whispered to myself.

I was about to go to my room when I got the strangest feeling. I walked to the back door and peered out. I couldn't see anything but the feeling was stronger and more forceful. All I could think about was following this invisible force.

I opened the door wider and slipped out into the fresh night air. I followed the tug as it pulled me from my house. It was as if something was urging me forward as easily as someone whispering directions in my ear. My legs followed the source straight into the thick of trees. I only stopped once as I tried to conjure a lamp of fire in my hands but all I got was sparks. I walked on until I knew exactly where I was headed.

When I reached the resting place I could tell where the power was radiating from straight away. There was a square patch of land almost at the border's edge and it was glowing. The glow was dull and faint, but it was there.

This was what had brought me here, without a doubt.

I walked closer and knelt at the edge of the glowing ground. I reached out my hand to touch it.

The ground erupted into a bright, white light that made me shield my eyes, and an ear-piercing shriek filled the area. I scrambled backwards trying to get as far away as possible. The further away I got, the less scary it became and it wasn't until I was on my feet and backing away that the shrieking stopped and the ground went back to its faint glow.

I stood rooted to the spot and unsure what I was waiting for, I turned and ran back towards home. I felt more confused and intrigued than I had before.

CHAPTER EIGHT
WILLOW

I had to clear my head upon waking. There was so much information swimming around that my brain was close to exploding.

I left the house quietly, careful not to wake Aspen, but when I headed to the thick of trees opposite the house Aspen cam strolling out.

"Where have you been?" I asked.

"I went for a walk." He said. "I did leave a note."

"Oh, I didn't notice. I'll be back in a bit, okay?"

"Sure, just don't go too far."

I took the familiar path through the forest that we took to get to Crownfire. The red and orange leaves crunching under my feet were comforting. The sun shining down was warm against my skin.

I reached the point where I had tripped on that first day. I was unsure whether I had imagined those air abilities. I hadn't shown any since and since I was over the shock of it now I wanted to try again.

The thick, dying branch was still lying on the floor partially covered with dirt and leaves. I couldn't sense any magic in the ground, so I concentrated hard to let the abilities show themselves.

No luck.

I continued to walk, thinking about what was different on that day. Maybe it was because I had tripped. If I made myself fall, maybe I could kickstart the ability.

I took a deep breath, closed my eyes and threw myself to the ground. I landed with a hard thud in the mud and leaves.

I got up and brushed myself off. This was ridiculous.

I got up and brushed myself off, and I threw myself to the ground again. I'm sure if someone was looking, they'd think I was crazy.

I wasn't going to try again. Maybe I had just imagined it after all. I had been tired, I hadn't slept much and I was worried about my parents and that insane meeting.

Suddenly, a huge gust of wind came out of nowhere and threw me backwards. I braced myself for a hard landing, but it didn't come.

I had done it. I hadn't imagined it. I was hovering about a foot off the ground staring up at the morning sky. I smiled to myself, and a few seconds later I dropped to the ground softly.

I lay on the ground for a few minutes, my body aching and tired. I felt drained. I got up, looked around, and then froze. Blue was standing just a few feet away, partly concealed by a large tree trunk.

"It was you, wasn't it? You blew me backwards." There was no sign of any breeze now. It had to be him.

"I had to," Blue said, walking towards me slowly. I knew that he had the ability of aerokinesis which meant he could manipulate the air and wind, but I didn't know he also had the ability of wind generation, which was how he blew me backwards.

"Why?"

"Look around you. Haven't you noticed where you are?"

I looked around and realised that I was at Crownfire. The flames were just inches away. If Blue hadn't been there…

"Oh, well thank you." I smiled at him.

"Don't you remember the Glacies story? Two boys thinking that they were indestructible. They thought that they could walk through Crownfire flames and live to tell the tale. It didn't end so well." Blue said.

"I remember. My parents used to drill it into us when we were younger."

"You should be more careful," Blue said.

"I will. I was just distracted. That's all."

Blue inclined his head in response. "Can I ask you something?" We were close now and I could see the turquoise in his eyes.

"Of course."

"How long have you had air abilities?"

I froze. He was a Tree Leader. He was the last person I could talk to about the extra abilities I was experiencing.

"I...I don't know what you mean?" I stammered. I silently cursed myself, I didn't sound very convincing.

Blue raised his eyebrows. "I saw you. You hovered. Not for long, but the ability is progressing." I looked down at the ground. I didn't know what to say. "One of my extra abilities is that I can sense other air users. I thought I sensed it in you, that day I came to Ignis. It was weak though, so I wasn't sure." Blue seemed to be thinking.

"I think you must be mistaken," I said forcefully.

Blue smiled kindly. "I'm sure now. In the few days that we haven't seen each other, your ability has strengthened. That's remarkable. Does your brother know?" he looked at me expectantly.

It would be pathetic to keep lying. "No, he doesn't. I didn't think it would be a good idea."

"That's smart. This stays between us."

I looked up at him. "You mean you're not going to say anything?"

Blue regarded me closely. "No. I won't say anything. There is a condition though. Will you tell me if you develop any of the other abilities of the elements. Have you noticed any of the earth or water abilities?"

"No, I haven't. I'll let you know if I do. It's nice to talk to someone about it though. Do you know what it means? I've never known anyone to have more than one elemental ability."

"Thank you." He seemed to be thinking. "I don't know, I'm afraid, however, I am going to do some research. If you need me, please meet me here. We can both be here freely and I'm usually hanging around. It's a bit quieter than in Ventus."

"Okay."

I expected him to teleport away, but instead, he walked around the edge of Crownfire and out of sight. He didn't even look back.

I was pleased. I could use air abilities and Blue had confirmed it. He seemed nice enough, but I was nervous too. I didn't know him well enough to know that he'd keep his word.

I thought about it all the way home, but I couldn't decipher him. I hadn't spent enough time around him to know him at all.

As I neared the house, Aspen came running out of the trees from the far side of the training ground. "Willow! Where have you been? I've been looking for you everywhere."

"Sorry, I was walking, and I didn't realise how far I had gone. It took me a little longer to get home than I thought." I said quickly.

Unexpectedly, Aspen threw his arms around me and pulled me into the tightest hug. "Aspen, what's wrong?" I said, shocked.

"I just don't what I'd do if I lose you too."

"You won't, and we haven't lost mom and dad so stop thinking like that."

Acacia was outside our house waiting for us when we got back home.

"Hi Acacia, what can we do for you?" I asked.

"I wondered if you had seen my brother?" I could tell that she had been crying, her eyes were red and puffy, and her breathing was short and gasping.

Aspen and I exchanged glances. "No, we haven't. When was the last time you saw him?" Aspen asked.

"I don't know. Mom was cold, so Forrest went to get some wood for the fire." She whimpered. "He never came back."

"How long ago was this?"

"Five hours, maybe more? We thought that he had just gone for a walk or something, but he never stays out in the thick after dark. Ever." Acacia was full-on crying now and threw herself into Aspen's arms. He patted her on the back awkwardly.

I couldn't help but smile, I knew that Acacia had had a crush on Aspen for a while now. He was oblivious of course.

When Acacia and Aspen had parted, Aspen announced that he was going to call a meeting with the Council.

"Don't worry," he said. "We're going to find out what happened. This can't be a coincidence."

I pulled Acacia into a hug. "It will be okay."

"Thanks." Acacia sniffed, tears still brimming her eyes. "I better go and tell mom about the meeting. Will you let us know what happens?"

"Of course."

I watched Acacia until she was safely back indoors and then joined my brother inside.

"Is it done?" I asked.

"Yes." He said. "The meeting is scheduled at first light. We'll leave here at about 5 am. Is that okay with you?"

I sat down at the table. "Of course. What's going on Aspen? Do you think the disappearances are linked?"

Aspen put his hand on my shoulder. "I do, but try not to think about it too much tonight."

I let out a short laugh. "That is going to be difficult."

"I know, but we need to try and get a bit of sleep so we are ready for the morning. Okay?"

I nodded, and Aspen squeezed my shoulder before leaving the kitchen to go to bed. I sighed and did the same.

CHAPTER NINE
WILLOW

I woke up shivering, the hairs on my arms raised. My mattress was soaking wet including my clothes and hair, which were all clung to my body. As I got out of bed and stood up, my feet squelched in the thick, grey, water-logged carpet.

"Aspen!" I shouted. He came running into the room, his green eyes wide. "What happened?" I asked, motioning around the room with my arms. He looked around.

"What do you mean?" he asked, clearly confused as his eyebrows wrinkled as he stared at me.

"Everything's wet, the carpet is ruined, the mattress is sopping, I'm soaked." I put my hands on my hips. "Seriously Aspen, open your eyes," I said impatiently.

"Willow, I don't see anything."

"What? Come here, stand right here." I demanded and watched as my brother came to stand where I stood. I heard his feet squelch into the carpet. He was barefoot.

"It's not wet, Willow." He repeated and turned to face me. "Are you feeling alright?"

I shook my head. "I don't understand."

"I'm going to go and make some breakfast. You should eat something." I answered with a nod. "We've got to leave soon."

Aspen left my room and all I could do was look around. I didn't know what was going on and decided to get ready as if nothing had happened. I was imagining it. I had to be.

Thirty minutes later, I was ready to go having flung on some trousers and a baggy top. I had ignored Aspen's remarks that it was too informal as we headed out the door and made our way to Crownfire.

"Willow, will you please pay attention to where you're going," Aspen said. He sounded irritated.

"Sorry," I said, catching up with my him. I was so distracted.

"What is wrong with you today? You're acting so strange."

"I don't know," I shrugged. Aspen gave me a quizzical look but continued to walk on. I breathed out a sigh of relief, I didn't need Aspen getting suspicious; suspicious of what though I wasn't so sure.

A few minutes later, we had arrived at Crownfire and I could distract myself with the meeting and my confused thoughts could be pushed to the back of my mind.

The other Tree Leaders were just arriving too. I watched Blue and Poppy appear from around the other side of Crownfire. Dune and Lily popped up out of the ground right in front of us. Dune gave us a friendly smile before following his wife to their platform. Oakley was already on his platform with Crimson. I found it strange that they weren't here before Aspen and me. They were always so punctual.

When we had taken our place on the platform and we were launched up to start the meeting, I noticed just how irritable the other Leaders looked. Oakley looked like he was ready to burst.

"Will somebody please tell me why we are here at this ungodly hour?" Oakley's voice boomed out. It echoed all around us. I flinched, knowing that it was entirely our fault.

I looked at my brother who rolled his eyes. "Someone else has gone missing from Ignis," he explained.

"When did this happen?" Dune asked.

"We were informed just after dark yesterday," Aspen said.

"Who is it that has gone missing?"

I looked around. Nobody looked particularly concerned.

"Our neighbour, Forrest. He's fifteen." Aspen explained. Ears started to prick up then.

"Fifteen?" Poppy asked incredulously.

"For goodness sake, he has probably just wandered off somewhere. It is what Youngers do," Oakley growled.

"You don't know what you're talking about!" I shouted so loud that the flames turned red around me. Everybody stared, I had surprised even myself. That was the first time I had ever spoken out at a meeting. Everyone was so shocked that nobody called me out on my rudeness.

"Anyway," Dune continued. "Is it possible that he did just wander off?"

"It's very out of character," Aspen explained.

"Extremely out of character," I piped up.

"Willow, be quiet," Aspen whispered, I bent my head, but not before getting a glimpse of Blue giving me a reassuring smile.

"Have you have had any contact from your parents yet?" Dune asked.

"Unfortunately, no. However, they were seen by Forrest and his sister Acacia the night they disappeared."

"Now Forrest has disappeared. I don't think that this is a coincidence." Dune said. "Where is Acacia now?"

"She's at home with her mother."

"Very well. I think that you need to keep a close eye on her."

"I agree," Aspen said.

"I'm curious, did Forrest say where he saw your parents?" Blue asked. I looked up quickly.

"He did," Aspen answered.

"Well, don't keep us in suspense boy," Oakley said, almost sarcastically.

"He pointed us in the direction of where they headed, and Willow and I followed the path. It led us to the outside border."

"Did you find anything?" Blue asked.

"No, nothing to suggest they were there at all," Aspen answered.

I was stunned that Aspen had kept Hazel's resting place to himself. He had said it so calmly that nobody would question it either.

"Are you going to do anything about these disappearances or not? Just standing there talking about it isn't helping, is it?" I said angrily.

"Willow!" Aspen growled under his breath.

"No, Aspen. I am getting sick of this now; something has got to be done." I looked around at the Tree Leaders. "What are you going to do?"

"Young lady, I think you need to calm down," Oakley said.

"Oh, you're one to talk, aren't you Oakley? When are you ever calm?" I was getting more and more worked up.

"I let your last bout of rudeness slip, but..."

"But what? What are you going to do?" I said and as I finished my sentence, I let the anger enclose me and then I heard Poppy and Lily scream. This is because I had suddenly gone up in flames. Not literally, of course. I was surrounded by flames, but for anyone watching, I would imagine it would look quite intense and severe.

"Willow, calm down!" I could barely hear Aspen's voice through the flames, but it was enough for me to use his voice to bring myself out of the state I was in. A moment later, the flames disappeared, and I was feeling a little flustered and slightly embarrassed. I looked around at the other Tree Leaders who all seemed to be speechless.

"I think it's time we were leaving, Aspen," I said as I ejected the platform to take us back to the ground.

"What was that, Willow? You just made us look like idiots." Aspen said as we disembarked off the platform.

"Not now, Aspen," I answered, already walking towards the thick of trees that would lead us home.

"Willow! Wait!" I turned to see Blue jogging towards us.

"What is it Blue?" I said sharply, still upset.

"I just wanted to see how you are. You became quite overwhelmed up there."

"I'm fine." I wasn't.

"Good," Blue said, turning to walk away. As he did, a light breeze blew over me and as it did, I heard Blue's voice. It was quiet, but it was there.

"Where did that breeze come from?" Aspen asked after Blue had left.

"No idea," I answered. I certainly couldn't tell my brother that it was a message from Blue and that I was meeting him back at Crownfire before dark.

Besides, I didn't want to tell him.

CHAPTER TEN
WILLOW

I was at Crownfire for around twenty minutes before Blue finally showed up.

"You took your time," I said.

"I said before dark, I didn't give a specific time."

I raised my eyebrows. He was correct, of course. "What did you want to talk to me about?" Blue smirked. "Who said I wanted to talk to you about anything?" he asked, still grinning.

"You did," I answered impatiently.

"I sent you a message to meet me here, not to talk," he said. "It was a sort of test."

"What do you mean?"

"I was seeing if you would show up, and then I would know for definite."

"You would know what for definite?" He was being extremely vague.

"I would know that you were an air user," he said. "Only those with air abilities would have heard that message I sent to you over the wind."

I raised my eyebrows. "You don't have to play games with me."

Blue lost his smirk. "Anyway," he said clearing his throat. "How is Acacia?"

"She's upset but fine. Thanks for asking." I smiled, it was still baffling to me that a Tree Leader was so compassionate; it was rare.

They were normally just out to protect themselves, but Blue was different.

Blue nodded in approval at my response. "Good."

"Why are you so nice?" I asked, but regretted the question as soon as I had asked it.

"You think I'm nice?" Blue replied, the smirk back on his face.

"Yes, I mean no, I mean…" I stammered. "What I mean is, that you seem to care. It's not usually the way of the Leaders."

Blue's smirk settled into a smile and then he looked thoughtful. "You're right, it is not the way of the Tree Leaders, but don't you think it should be?"

"I do," I answered.

"I'm glad we agree. You are one of us now." Blue stated.

"Temporarily." I corrected him.

"Right," Blue said, smiling. I didn't know what it was, but I suddenly felt completely at ease around him, almost like I could tell him anything.

We sat down on the ground, sitting back against one of the tree trunks.

"I love this side of the Centre," Blue said, twirling a piece of grass in-between his fingers. "There's never any leaves on the ground in Ventus."

"None at all?" I asked. I couldn't imagine my life without the sound of the leaves crunching and crackling around me.

"No, there's a lot of blossom covering the ground, but no leaves."

"Wow, I bet that's so pretty."

"I guess. When you see it every day, you just get used to it though. It's nothing special." Blue shrugged.

"Really? I don't think I could ever get bored with the leaves in Ignis. They are so beautiful, especially when the sun is setting. Our Zone wouldn't be the same without them. Don't you think that would be the same in Ventus, without the blossom?"

"I guess I just believe that it's the people that make the community, not whatever is on the ground."

I thought about that in silence for a while. "Blue?"

"Hmm?" He was lying on the ground with his hands behind his head. It was starting to go dark and I could see the leaves start to glow on the ground around him as the sun began to set.

"Can I tell you something?" I asked.

"Sure, what is it?" Blue continued to lie down, his eyes closed. It would be easier, I thought, to explain when he wasn't looking at me.

"Something happened this morning, and I'm not sure whether I imagined it or whether it happened. Aspen said he couldn't see anything."

"What happened?" He lifted himself on to his elbows so that he was looking at me.

"When I woke up this morning, the bed, the floor, everything, was soaking wet. I could feel and hear my feet squelching on the carpet and when Aspen came in, he said that nothing was wrong."

"Okay," Blue said, listening.

"What I want to know is, is this the start of water abilities showing? If I have air abilities on top of my fire element, isn't it possible that I could be a water user too?" I asked.

"I think that it is very possible. The only abilities that you should have are fire. Your parents are both from the fire elemental lineage, which means there is no reason for you not to be. Since you are showing signs of an air user too, I think you can expect abilities from all elements."

"All elements?" I asked quietly.

"Yes."

"How is that possible?"

"It is rare, but not unheard of." He said softly. "Willow, I don't think this conversation should be repeated. People wouldn't understand."

I nodded. I already knew that I shouldn't mention the fact that I could work with the other elements.

"Why couldn't Aspen see or feel the water in my room?"

"I think that your subconscious knew that you couldn't even tell your brother. You could have sent signals to him to make him not see it if you know what I mean."

"I'm so confused," I said, falling back so that I was lying on the ground next to Blue. The leaves crunched beneath me, and I put an arm over my face to block out the world.

We lay in silence for a while. There wasn't much noise other than a slight breeze and the distant sounds of insects.

"Willow, you need to be prepared."

"Prepared for what?"

"Prepared for the fact that in two days you turn eighteen. Then all these abilities are going to be so much more powerful than they are right now. For someone with just one ability, it is a challenge. For someone with all four elemental abilities, I cannot even begin to imagine."

"The way I see it is that I wouldn't have these abilities if I was unable to control them. I have to believe that." I said.

"That's a good way to think about it Willow," Blue said.

I smiled.

CHAPTER ELEVEN
WILLOW

"Willow." The voice was quiet and sounded very far away, barely a whisper. "Willow."

I knew who it was, and instantly the voice was a calming, comforting effect, which soon gave way to a resounding fear.

My mother was trying to reach out to me.

"Mom, where are you?" I shouted, my voice echoed around me. I didn't know where I was. It was dark, and the ground was hard and jagged beneath my feet like I was walking on small rocks.

"Willow." The voice sounded closer now, but maybe it was just my imagination. I kept walking with my hands out in front of me, hoping that I wouldn't walk into anything.

I shivered as I walked, I wasn't sure whether it was the cold or fear.

"Willow." I jumped, the hairs on the back of my neck rising. The voice was a whisper, right in my ear. I spun around, waving my arms as I did, but I couldn't feel anyone there. I couldn't sense anyone either, there was no noise other than hearing myself breathe and my footsteps.

Ahead of me, a fire erupted, and although I was used to flames, the sight of it shocked me.

"Willow!" My mother's voice was so loud that it echoed around me.

"Mom!" I shouted, and without thinking, I ran towards the fire. I was so close that the flames were licking my skin, burning along with the clothes on my back. I could feel the heat intensely but I couldn't feel any pain.

I woke up in my bed, my body sweating. Hot flames surrounded me, and Aspen was in the doorway screaming my name.

"Willow!" Aspen was just the other side of the flames, using his ability to try and extinguish them; it wasn't working though.

I jumped through the flames, dousing them as I did. My mind was still transfixed on what I had just seen. "We have to help mom, Aspen," I said as I ran into my closet to pull on a pair of jeans and a sweatshirt.

"Willow, what are you talking about?" Aspen asked, his voice sounding panicked.

"Now Aspen!" I shouted as I stormed back into the room.

"Willow, stop!" Aspen shouted and just as I was about to leave the room, the doorway was blocked by a wall of flames and I found myself trapped.

"Aspen, remove them."

"Not until you tell me what is going on."

"We don't have time for this," I shouted. As I did, I turned back towards the flames which immediately disappeared, and I flew through the door.

"What the..." Aspen said, shocked. "How did you do that?" I ignored him, but I could hear him running after me.

I had left the house in a blur, and I ran towards the trees, their branches hiding me from view. Aspen was calling out for me but his voice was getting further and further away. I knew exactly where to go and even though blackness surrounded me, I knew the direction as if it was written on the back of my hand.

I kept running, that invisible pull urging me on like before. Aspen's calls were gone now, too far away for me to hear.

I finally made it into the clearing, just short of the outside border. I knew that I was in the right place as soon as I stepped onto the ground surrounding Hazel's resting place. I could feel the power.

I walked over to it and stepped onto the glowing ground. Lightning struck, and I was thrown backwards. I landed heavily against a large tree trunk, the breath was knocked out of me, and I doubled over holding my stomach. I couldn't stop myself from coughing.

I stood up slowly. My hand rested on the gnarled tree and I used it to centre my body before I walked back over to the resting place. I was astonished to see small sparks at the end of my fingertips. It looked as if an electrical current was flowing through me.

I was sure that this had something to do with Hazel. I walked forward, more determined than ever to find out what was happening. In my current headspace, I didn't notice the very large rock jutting out from the ground, and I fell forwards. I barely had time to brace myself for the landing.

As I fell, my arms flew upward of their own accord, and I was surged skywards before I had the chance to hit the ground. I stopped breathing as a lightning bolt shot out of my finger. The pain in my hand was indescribable as the bolt connected with the sky.

The sky lit up a bright white, and the loudest clap of thunder sounded around the bolt of lightning. I was suspended between standing and falling, the connection keeping me from plummeting to the ground.

I could feel myself becoming weaker and when I felt like my body couldn't endure anymore, the connection broke. I could barely register the fall and then I was on the ground.

CHAPTER TWELVE
BLUE

I got up off the swinging seat in front of my house. After talking with Willow, I found the blossom, shimmering delicately in the moonlight, a gift. It was something that I always took for granted and I had finally come to realise that maybe it wouldn't always be this way.

I had been outside for a good while. I loved how quiet it was which made it a great place to think. As I got up to go inside, a flicker in the sky caught my eye. I squinted in the direction. It had been faint and only lasted a few seconds. It was probably nothing, but it didn't sit right.

I took in a deep breath and concentrated on what I was to do. I could feel it before it happened, as always. A cold, vacuum-like sensation enveloped my body as I twisted in on myself. I screwed my eyes shut and thought of my destination. Seconds later, I landed with a soft thud, slightly unbalanced, on the mountain training ground.

The training ground was quiet, and the clouds thick with fog. I looked in the direction of what I had seen just a few moments ago. The sky was dark again. Nothing seemed out of place, but as I was about to leave, a lightning bolt appeared in the distance. It didn't disappear, it was as though it was frozen in place. My gut was screaming at me that something was amiss. The lightning bolt looked as if it was in Ignis and I knew I wouldn't be able to enter the Zone unnoticed.

I concentrated hard until the flapping of its wings sent a breeze through my hair. I opened my eyes to find the Sylph flapping its wings in place, waiting for me to climb on. As I did, its body and a head full of white and silver feathers disappeared beneath me. The Sylph was an invisible being of the sky and made flying on it that much more fun.

I directed the Sylph towards the lightning. As I got closer, the light in the sky seemed to differ and the bolt disappeared. I continued to fly towards where I had seen it last. I circled high looking down. I was above the outside border. Something dark was on the ground, unmoving. As I slowly spiralled downwards, the figure became bolder. I knew who it was before I reached the ground.

"Willow?" I called down to her, but she didn't stir. I jumped off the Sylph. It disappeared into a whirlwind, blowing me gently down towards her. "Willow?"

I knelt next to her. She was freezing to touch, but she was breathing. I lifted her into my arms and began running through the trees towards the Ignis community. Now and again, red eyes stared at me as I moved through the thick. I ignored them and carried on running. My father had always told me that the Superno was more scared of you than you were of them. I'm not sure I ever really believed him, but they seemed to be keeping their distance.

"Willow?" I heard a seemingly familiar voice calling out through the forest. I slowed to a walk, deciphering from which direction the voice was coming from.

"Over here," I shouted. I walked toward the voice and a few moments later, Aspen came running through the trees.

"What happened?" Aspen said as he hurried over, his eyes wide. "Is she…"

"She's fine, I think. She is breathing at least." I said. I heard Aspen let out an audible sigh.

"What happened?" he repeated.

"I have no idea, to be honest," I said. "I saw a bolt of lightning, it seemed a little strange and I went to check it out. That is when I found her."

"She ran off," Aspen explained. "She seemed like she was on a mission. She was screaming that we needed to help our mom."

"Let's just get her home, okay?" I said.

Aspen nodded and led the way.

CHAPTER THIRTEEN
WILLOW

When I opened my eyes, it was hazy. I couldn't make sense of where I was. It was warm though, compared to the icy cold that had enveloped my body when the lightning struck.

"Where am I?" I said, shocked to hear myself slurring.

"Willow!" Aspen shouted. "Thank goodness." I felt him take my hand. It was warm. My eyes had closed, they felt heavy, and I was struggling to open them.

"Where am I?" I repeated.

"You're at home," Aspen said, with slight hysteria in his voice.

The panic in his voice scared me. "How did I get home?"

"Blue found you collapsed in the forest," Aspen answered. "He carried you back."

"Blue's here?"

"He's just outside. He didn't think it would be appropriate to be in your bedroom."

"You should take a leaf out of his book," I said with a small smile.

"Maybe, but right now, I'm staying. You scared the hell out of me Willow." He said. I felt sorry for him. If I were in his position, I would probably be a little freaked out by my behaviour too.

"How long was I out for?" I asked.

"A few hours."

"What!?" I struggled to sit up, but Aspen was holding me down. "Aspen, let go!"

"Willow, no! You need to rest." He shouted back at me.

"I am fine," I said through gritted teeth. The truth was, I had never felt worse. My head was pounding, and my body was so tired that I wasn't even sure that I could stand up without my legs collapsing beneath me.

It didn't take long for me to fall back on the bed in defeat. My body spent.

Aspen sat down at the end of the bed, then there was a soft knock at the door.

"Is everything okay?" Blue's voice was muffled through the door.

"We are fine," I said.

"Then would it be okay if I had a word?" Blue asked.

Aspen got up off the bed and opened the bedroom door. Blue was standing there in a black sweatshirt with matching bottoms, looking slightly uncomfortable. I had never seen him dressed in such casual clothes.

"You can come in," Aspen said, returning to my bed.

"May I?" Blue said, looking to me for approval.

"Yes, of course," I said.

Satisfied, Blue stepped into the room. I gestured to the desk chair that was situated next to the bed and he sat down.

"Thank you."

There was a short silence. "What did you want to talk to me about?" I asked.

"About what happened out there."

I looked at my brother. "Aspen, can you give us a minute?"

"But, Willow…"

"Aspen, please," I said cutting him off. He looked as if he was about to protest, but he grudgingly got up off the bed and walked out of the room, slamming the door as he did so.

"Sorry," I apologised, embarrassed.

"Don't be," Blue said. "I would act the same way if I were in his position."

"It's not fair on him though. He just wants to help. He is scared and I'm not making it any better. I just wish I could tell him, but to be honest, I don't know how he would react."

Blue looked thoughtful. "I think its best if you don't tell him. It's easier, at least for now."

I nodded. "What did you see out there, you know, when you found me?"

"Nothing. I found you collapsed on the floor. What happened, Willow?"

I looked at him, I didn't know if I should tell him. Yes, he knew about everything else, but this was so much bigger than all of that, but I had to tell someone. I was going to Awaken in a few hours and I didn't know what was going to happen.

"It's strange. I'm not sure how to explain it." I admitted.

"That's okay. Just take your time." Blue sat back in his chair waiting for me to return to what I was saying.

"Okay, I'm scared to say it, Blue. I don't know how you are going to react to this. It's not like the elemental abilities that we all know about. This is more, a lot more, and I'm frightened that you are going to be all weird about it.' I was rambling. I looked down at my hands, twiddling my thumbs, and waited for Blue to say something.

"Willow, there is nothing you can say that is going to freak me out. I'm not going to walk away."

"You're just saying that because you have to. You're a Tree Leader. It's your job."

"That might be, but you are my friend Willow and I'm going to stick around and help you whether you like it or not. In just a few hours, you are going to need my help."

"I'm going to need your help with what?" I asked.

"Your turning eighteen, and I have a feeling that it's not going to be the same as the usual Awakening. Yours is going to be a powerful one and I am going to be there for you to help you through it." Blue said.

He leant forward in his chair and took my hand in his. He was warm to touch, and a tingling travelled up my arm. I pulled my hand away and Blue sat back again in his chair, looking a little embarrassed.

"Are you going to continue your story?" He asked.

I took a deep breath. "Okay, well I ran towards Hazels resting place because I don't know, something was pulling me there, I guess. When I got there, I could feel the power radiating around the area. I don't know how I just felt it." I said, looking at Blue. He didn't say anything; he just gave me a look as if to say, 'carry on'.

I looked away as I said the next thing. "I don't remember how exactly, but lightning struck the ground near to where I was standing, and it knocked me backwards. I landed on the other side of the clearing."

"Is that when I found you?" Blue asked.

"Not exactly."

"Go on." Blue urged.

"I walked back towards the middle of the clearing and tripped over a rock. As I was falling…" I sighed. "This is ridiculous." I went silent for a moment. I looked at Blue. He was waiting for me to carry on. "When I fell, a lightning bolt shot out of my finger towards the sky." I looked at Blue, trying to see his reaction. He didn't say or do anything to suggest that he was completely freaked over the idea that the girl in front of him had an electrical current running through her body.

"What happened then?" he asked, nodding his head.

"Then it's like the bolt that came out of my finger connected with the sky somehow, and it stopped me from falling. It's like I was suspended in mid-air and the connection was keeping me up. I remember the lightning in the sky and this huge thunderclap and then I fell. I don't remember anything else."

Blue sat there without saying a word. He seemed to be deep in thought.

"Electrokinesis," Blue murmured.

"Electro what?" I hadn't heard of it before.

"Electrokinesis," Blue said, a little louder this time. "It is the ability to control, generate or absorb electric fields and shoot lightning bolts."

"How is that even possible?" I asked. "You'd still need training to perform abilities like that, and I've never done that before in my life."

We were both quiet for a moment. "Why aren't you running away?" I asked quietly.

"I said I wouldn't, didn't I?" Blue said.

"I guess. I just didn't think that you'd stay in the presence of a crazy person." Blue chuckled to himself. "You see, I knew you wouldn't believe me."

"Willow, I wasn't laughing because I don't believe you, and I don't think that you are crazy either."

"Then why did you laugh?"

"I laughed because I can't believe that you don't trust me. After everything I've said to you, you still think that I'm going to bail on you." Blue got up from the chair, moving to sit on the edge of the bed. I froze as he did so, unsure of what to do. "I'm here for you, no matter what. I need you to believe that. I need you to trust me."

I nodded. "I think I do. Trust you, I mean." Blue nodded and got up off the bed.

"Good," Blue said smiling. "I'm glad." He walked towards the door. "I am going to go and get changed, but I'll be back before you Awaken."

"Blue?"

"Yeah?"

"How did you find me? How did you know something was wrong?" I asked.

"I'm not sure," he said thoughtfully. "I saw the lightning, but I guess I kind of had this feeling. Sort of like you were calling out for me. Were you?"

I shook my head. "Not that I remember."

"Anyway, I flew straight to Ignis. The closer I got to you, the more I could sense the air user within you. I knew it was you before I landed."

"Well, thank you for looking out for me. I appreciate it." I said smiling.

"No problem," he said, walking towards the door. "I'll see you soon."

As soon as Blue left, Aspen burst into my room.

"Knock much?" I scowled.

"Sorry," he said, not looking sorry at all, I thought. "So, what was all that about?" he asked, sitting down on the end of my bed.

"Nothing," I said, turning away from him.

"I wonder why the warning trigger didn't alert anyone to Blue's presence?" Aspen wondered out loud. I shifted uncomfortably. He looked at me. "What is it?"

"Well, since I became a Tree Leader, I've found that there are a few things I can do now that I couldn't do before."

"Like what?" Aspen asked.

"Like turning off the trigger system…" I answered.

"How?"

"Well, I was thinking about it and –"

Aspen put his hand up to stop me. "Wait, why were you thinking about it?"

"Oh, well no reason," I replied hastily.

Aspen looked sceptical. "Carry on, how did you do it?" he urged.

"That's just the thing, I was thinking about it, and I kind of just felt this weird sensation and I knew I had done it." I shrugged and looked at Aspen, waiting for his reaction.

"I'm going to go and get some fresh air." He got up and left the room and I just stared after him. I had no idea what he was thinking.

CHAPTER FOURTEEN
BLUE

Walking back through the thick gave me time to think. The sun had started to rise, illuminating the trees slightly. Seeing Willow lying in bed like that, seeming so weak and deflated, made *me* feel weak. I had this overwhelming urge to protect her, and I had failed.

I was walking towards Crownfire. The neutral ground there radiated with power and I needed that right now. I needed to feel powerful, instead of useless. As I approached the Centre, I couldn't help but picture that lightning bolt in my head. I didn't know what it meant.

"Blue." The soft voice shook me out of my thoughts.

"Poppy. What are you doing here?" I asked. It was still dark.

"I was worried. I woke up to get some water and I noticed that you were gone." Poppy explained. Now I felt guilty on top of everything else.

"I'm sorry. How did you know I would be here?"

Poppy smirked. "Really? You're always here."

"Right." I sat down on the ground, my back against a particularly large tree trunk. Poppy followed suit. Her face was pale, and her eyes were big and wide.

"What's wrong? This isn't like you," she said. I looked my sister in the eyes, the same blue as my own. "You are always a happy one. The optimistic one. You find the good in everyone and everything.

Now you are sitting here looking like you've lost everything in the world."

I put my arm around my sister's shoulders and she leaned against me. "I'm fine. There is just a lot going on right now, and I don't know what to do about it."

"Is this something to do with that Ignis girl'" Poppy asked.

I smiled. "Her name is Willow, and yes, it is partly to do with her."

"Just be careful, Blue. I don't want to see you getting hurt." I tightened my grip around her. Poppy was only three years younger than me, but I still saw her as the little girl I ended up raising after our parents died.

"I've missed this," she said. "We don't spend much time together anymore."

"We should rectify that," I said. I felt Poppy nod her head. "Come on. Let's go home." I held my hand out to help my sister up off the ground. "My gosh, you're getting heavy," I joked as I pulled her up.

"Jerk," Poppy retorted, giving me a shove. We both laughed. "Let's walk, okay?"

"Sure."

CHAPTER FIFTEEN
WILLOW

I slid my legs over the side of the bed and lifted myself into a sitting position. It was tiring, my whole body felt heavy as if I were trying to move through water.

Gingerly, I put my feet on the ground and tested my weight. It seemed okay. I stood up slowly. My body felt as if it was going to collapse beneath me, but thankfully I stood steady.

I went over to the mirror and gasped. I looked ill. My face was pale white and there were black circles around my eyes. My hair looked as if I had never run a brush through it in my life and my clothes were covered in mud. The worst thing of all though was that I couldn't believe that I had been lying in bed looking like I had in front of Blue.

I opened my bedroom door to the usual quiet that I had come to expect. Aspen was still out somewhere. I didn't expect him back anytime soon; he had always been so dramatic.

I sat down at the kitchen table leaning forward so that my head was resting on my arms. The Awakening was happening soon; I could feel it. The power was itching to appear, and it felt like someone was inside of me, slowly pushing through every part of my body.

The sweat was pouring from me and I took deep breaths as a sharp pain seemed to reverberate through my entire body. My mother would tell me to breathe in through my nose and out through my mouth. It wasn't working.

I started to feel shivery and I reached for the glass on the table. Slowly, it started to fill with water. I raised my eyebrows, the pain momentarily replaced with curiosity, and watched with wonder as it the glass filled and filled. As it reached the brim of the glass the water turned to ice.

I gasped. Oakley was the only person powerful enough in Glacies to manipulate ice. This couldn't be happening.

My eyes widened as the ice expanded, and I only had just enough time to shield my face before the glass shattered. I winced as the shards of ice and glass hit my bare arms.

My mother would know what to do. She would know if it was normal. I couldn't stop the tears from appearing in my eyes. I was alone.

A pain in my chest pulled me from my thoughts. I clutched at my throat as I struggled to breathe. I could barely get out a breath, each one getting harder and shallower. I thought I was going to pass out from the lack of oxygen. I could feel myself getting dizzy, and my body felt weaker than ever.

I hadn't realised that I had fallen until I was on the floor. The chair was lying on the floor next to me. My eyes began to close and I could start to see stars in front of my eyes, and just when I thought that this was the end, it was as if somebody released me and I took a huge breath, my lungs filling with air.

On my second breath, my body left the ground until I was hovering so high off the floor that my hands were touching the ceiling. As much as I tried, I couldn't bring myself back to the ground. I tried to push off the ceiling with my feet, but my body was too weak.

I could feel the flames licking my body. It had become such a familiar feeling to me that I anticipated it welcomingly.

I knew this.

I looked forward to it.

CHAPTER SIXTEEN
BLUE

I heard the commotion as soon as I entered the Ignis community ground. There was a lot of people wandering around, but mostly they were staring towards Willow's house.

"Everybody, you need to get back inside your homes," I said this with authority and nobody questioned me.

I walked closer to the house and peered through the window. Willow was going through the Awakening but I knew better than to disturb the process. It could do more harm than good if I interrupted her.

I watched in wonder and fear as she went through the motions. As she was lifted into the air I was certain that that was the air abilities manifesting. I had gone through something similar during my Awakening.

When Willow's elemental fire ability manifested I had to stop myself from screaming out. My eyes were wide with what I was seeing. I had never seen it before in my lifetime.

Slowly, Willow lowered to the ground where she landed softly, picked up the fallen chair and collapsed into it. It was only then that the flames disappeared.

I walked around to the door and knocked quietly before walking inside.

Willow turned to me. "How long have you been there?" she asked.

I studied her carefully. "Somewhere between you hovering in mid-air to you erupting into flames."

"That was just the half of it."

"What happened?" I asked. I bent down to put the table right which had upturned and then sat down opposite Willow.

"Let's see. I conjured water, turned it to ice, lifted into the air and then erupted into flames. I think that's about it." She looked at me and it took all my strength to stay on my side of the table.

"Wow." It was all I could say.

"Blue?"

"Yeah?"

"Is this normal?" she asked quietly.

I considered my words carefully. "When somebody Awakens their ability manifests and shows you just how powerful you are. From what you have told and what I have seen, I believe that you have Awakened with the abilities of all four elements."

"Four?" she asked. "I've only shown signs of three."

I stood up. "Follow me."

I led Willow outside. The sight was baffling to me so when I heard Willow freeze in the doorway behind me, I knew that she was just as baffled.

The garden outside, and those of the neighbouring community, were covered in beautiful flowers, in all the colours you could imagine; reds, yellows and blues.

"What happened? Ignis has never had flowers. This looks more like Terra." Willow was gaping at the colourful display.

"I'm pretty sure that you had something to do with this," I said.

"How? How did I do all this without even knowing it?" she asked.

I shook my head. "I have no idea. There is something else you should know too. Let's go back inside."

I went inside and Willow followed close behind me.

"What is it?" she asked as she sat back down at the table.

"When I came in and you burst into flames…" I started.

"'Can I just say, that I don't burst into flames. The flames just surround me, like they're protecting me." She argued.

"Okay, when the flames surrounded you, I couldn't help but notice that they were purple."

"What was purple?" Willow asked, confused.

"The flames," I said.

Willow laughed. "Don't be silly."

"I'm not joking, Willow. Its why I was so shocked."

"Seriously? After everything that has happened and is happening to me, that is what shocks you? Why?"

"Purple is a sign of necromancy magic, Willow."

"But that's impossible."

"Not if your parents have necromancy magic in their blood." I pointed out.

"Okay, but let's say that they did. Wouldn't they produce purple flames? Wouldn't Aspen?" she argued.

"Well, I would have thought so, yes," I said.

"Well, then what you are saying is wrong because I have never known any of them to produce purple flames. Maybe it was your imagination?"

"I don't think so."

"There is one other thing," I said. "It seems that your eyes have changed colour today. They are a very light purple."

We both sat in silence. I had a feeling that I had upset Willow, and I didn't want to make it worse. I didn't know Willow's family well enough, or her extended family, and there was every chance that she was loosely related to somebody with necromancy blood.

"Have you seen my brother?" Willow asked after a while. She said nothing about her eyes.

"I haven't. is he not here?"

I looked around expecting Aspen to appear from down the hallway.

"I haven't seen him since he left my bedroom after we talked." She said. "He knew that I was about to Awaken. He would never leave for this long."

I understood her frustration. She was getting worked up and it was no wonder after all she had been through.

"I'm sure he has just lost track of time."

"Maybe," she said. "You know, somebody could have told me how painful it was to Awaken. I never want to be in that much pain again." Willow thought for a moment, one eyebrow up and her eyes focusing on something I couldn't make out. "If it is so important, then why isn't there some big ceremony or something? Why isn't there a bigger deal made from it?"

"The Zones used to make a huge deal about them. When someone was about to Awaken, everyone from the community and the Tree Council would gather around to be there for them and to witness that person's true ability for the first time." I explained.

"Why did all of that stop?"

"I'm not sure exactly."

CHAPTER SEVENTEEN
WILLOW

Blue had stayed for a cup of tea after we talked and I introduced him to liquorice root. He had never had it before, and I don't think I would ever forget the way he screwed his face up after the first sip. Suffice to say that he won't be having it again.

I hadn't felt so alone when in his company, and now the silence was overwhelming.

The silence gave me time to think of all the questions that I needed answers too. I wasn't ready for them. I still had to come to terms that I had Awoken with abilities from all four Zones. The Tree Council would be furious that I hadn't shared this information with them, despite Blue's reassurances that I didn't need to.

I looked outside again through the gap in the curtains. I was expecting my brother to appear from in the thick full of apologies, but the Zone was quiet.

I went to bed despite not being tired, but I knew that my body was spent. It needed to rest, whether I wanted to or not.

CHAPTER EIGHTEEN
BLUE

I left Willow's house feeling more confused than I did before. My mind was reeling, how could Aspen leave her alone? Willow needed her parents right now and since they were missing, all she had was her brother, and he had left her.

I began to walk straight into the forest to find him when I noticed a young girl leaving her house and making her way to Willow's. She looked upset.

"Excuse me?" I called over. The girl stopped short and looked over at me.

"Blue?" she asked quietly. I walked over to her.

"That's right. What's your name?" I asked. "Are you okay?"

"I'm Acacia. I just really needed to talk to Willow."

I nodded my head. If I could remember rightly, this was Forrest's sister. The boy who went missing. "Willow needs her rest right now. Maybe I would do?" I waited for her reaction. She seemed to be weighing up the offer. After a moment or two, she slowly nodded her head.

"Okay."

"Why don't we sit down then," I said, gesturing to the giant logs situated around the campfire. I waited until we were both sitting. Acacia was staring straight ahead. "So, what did you want to talk to Willow about?"

"I just wanted to ask her if she has heard anything about my brother."

"Forrest, right?" Acacia nodded. "As far as I am aware, there is no news yet." I could see the tears forming as I said those words.

"He's gone, isn't he?" she sobbed.

I put my hands on her shoulders and turned her towards me. "Look, no news is good news, okay? There is nothing to suggest that Forrest is gone. You just have to have faith." Acacia looked at me, her eyes were red and swollen. She nodded.

"I suppose I better go back to my mom."

"How is she doing?" I asked.

"She is hanging in there, thanks for asking." There was a small smile on her lips. "I think she is in denial. She just thinks that he'll walk through the door at any moment."

"Well, maybe he will," I said. "Look after your mom, okay? You'll always need her."

"I will, thank you Blue."

I watched Acacia walk to her door. She glanced back once she got there, looking slightly happier than she had when she had first left the house. I was glad of the fact that I had comforted her if only a little.

I looked over my shoulder at Willow's front door. She had a long journey ahead of her, and I was amazed at how she was handling it.

CHAPTER NINETEEN
WILLOW

I hadn't felt like I'd been asleep long when I heard a knock at the door. My body ached and groaned as I forced myself to sit up, and the door knocked again as I made my way down the hall.

"I'm coming," I shouted, although it came out quieter than I wanted it to. I suddenly realised how quiet it was. I could tell that the sun would be rising soon due to the soft glow out of the window, but I hadn't expected the silence that came with it. I couldn't even hear the birds.

I reached the door and pulled it open. I gasped and stared at a tunnel. I couldn't see the end of it but it was clear this was a dream.

It was almost pitch black apart from the glowing light that emanated from below the ground. It was a bridge and flames licked the edges of the pathway lighting up the cave-like walls. I slowly began to walk down the path with the strangest feeling that I had walked through this tunnel before.

The further I walked along the tunnel, the further it seemed to spread out in front of me. I carried on walking though, the desire to find out where the tunnel led was burning through my body. I still couldn't see the end, the tunnel was twisting and turning and as I looked behind me, I could no longer see the house.

I came to a fork in the pathway. I stopped, trying to decide which way to go. Both were identical, and both were mysteries as to where they led. I turned right and walked on.

There was a very faint light ahead of me, but I wasn't sure if it was my imagination. I was trying so hard to focus on something in the darkness that I couldn't be certain that it was real.

The light began to brighten and I sped up a little.

As I reached the ending of the tunnel, I cautiously and quietly crept towards it. I gaped when I realised what I had discovered. It was the inside of a gigantic cave and it could have fit into my entire house fifty times or more. The thing that shocked me the most though was the people that I could see. There were maybe a hundred people, all just sitting around in groups, some on their own. They were not full people though; I couldn't describe it. I could see straight through them like they were part invisible.

I looked around, I didn't recognise any of them from what I could see. I couldn't even approach them, the exit or entrance from where I stood had no way of getting down to the ground, it was just a sheer drop of maybe fifty feet and I had no intention of trying to get down there.

The silence was broken when I heard the most terrifying cackle that echoed down the tunnel behind me. The hairs on the back of my neck shot up, and goosebumps covered my arms. There was a huge blast of icy cold air that knocked me back against the cave wall where I hit my head. I was too dizzy to stand which was made worse when I discovered the blood seeping from the back of my head.

I could feel myself growing weaker and my legs were threatening to buckle underneath me. I slumped on the ground a bit further feeling my eyelids grow heavy. Through the slit I could see in my vision I thought I saw a woman ahead of me in the darkness.

My eyes shut completely.

I awoke gasping for breath. I flailed my arms around me, the image of the woman fresh in my mind. I became confused though when I realised where I was. I was lying in bed, in the same position as I was when I had laid down earlier.

I couldn't think. I sat up and looked out of the window. It was starting to grow dark and I had no idea how long I had slept for.

I lay back down on the pillow only to discover a sharp pain on the back of my head. I reached around to touch and noticed my hand covered in dry blood. I raised my eyebrows and my heart began to thump a little faster. Had the tunnel dream been real?

I got out of bed gingerly, staggering slightly, but when I was sure I would be able to walk unaided, I walked out into the hallway and towards the outside door in the kitchen. I opened the door partially, peering around the frame. The tunnel was gone, and the garden was there as it should be.

***

The next morning I discovered that Aspen had still not returned. I had tossed and turned for the rest of the night, and I was determined that the answers lay at the outside border. I didn't know why I was the only one that could feel its power, but it had to mean something.

I left the house in a blur and walked towards Crownfire with the hope of meeting Blue there. When I arrived it was still quiet and so I settled myself on the ground against our tree.

I felt safe in the area surrounding Crownfire. The neutral ground was a haven for everybody, and there was no tension in the air. I felt safe enough that my body just broke down, and once the tears started, it was difficult to stop.

A hand squeezed my shoulder and I jumped in surprise. I looked up expecting to see Blue, but instead, his sister Poppy was staring down at me. I frantically wiped at my face, trying to compose myself as she sat down beside me.

"Are you okay?" she asked.

I couldn't even answer her, every time I tried to open my mouth to talk, I nearly burst out crying again. I simply shrugged my shoulders in response, hoping that was an acceptable response.

"Don't worry," Poppy said. "You don't have to talk if you don't want to." Poppy stayed sitting. I was sort of glad to have some company, even though I felt embarrassed about the state I was in.

"I bet you were expecting my brother, weren't you? I'm sure he will be here soon. He's taken a shine to you Willow. He normally doesn't get so invested in people from other Zones."

"Really?" I had found my voice. It was shaky, but there.

"Sure."

"It's wrong though," I said. "People from different Zones are not supposed to interact socially."

I had been thinking about it for a while now, ever since Blue had shown up in Ignis. If the other Tree Leaders found out that we had been communicating outside of council meetings, all hell would break loose.

"This is true." Poppy said. "However, if you knew my brother as well as I do, you would know that he doesn't care about all that stuff. He wants the ways of our people to change."

I nodded. he had said something similar before about how the council acted. I agreed, of course.

"What are you doing here, anyway? Is there another council meeting?" I asked.

Poppy chuckled. She sounded very like her brother. "There's no meeting," she said. "My brother is not the only one that likes to go for walks." She looked around her. "There's something very calming about this place."

"I agree. I feel very safe here. I'm not sure why though."

Poppy nodded her head in agreement. "I think it has something to do with the magic surrounding Crownfire. The abilities of all four elements combine within Crownfire. The powers work together, and I guess that sends off a unique signal, creating a calm, harmonic effect."

"That sounds amazing."

Poppy nodded. "It does."

The leaves around us began to swirl around our bodies. I looked around in amazement, but when I looked at Poppy, expecting her to show the same shocked expression, Poppy just looked bored.

"Relax," she said. "It's just my brother showing off as usual." I looked around and sure enough, Blue stepped out from behind a tree, with a huge grin on his face.

"Thanks, sis, you had to ruin it, didn't you?" Blue said jokingly.

"Oh Blue, she would have figured out it was you eventually."

"Maybe so," Blue said as he plonked himself down beside us. "What has she been saying about me then?" he asked me.

"Nothing much," I replied. Blue looked at me then, concern slowly growing on his face.

"What's the matter?" He was looking at my face. I could just imagine what I looked like, my face always went red and puffy when I had been crying.

"Nothing. I'm fine." I replied.

"Yeah, right. Tell me." he insisted.

"Leave her alone, Blue. She will tell you if, and when she wants to." Poppy argued.

Blue backed off and sat back against the tree. We all sat there quietly for a while, the breeze blowing gently around us. Poppy was making a small leaf hover over her palm and Blue was attempting to blow it away, without much luck. The air element must work much like the fire element where only the conjurer can control his or her ability. I wished that I could control my abilities as well as the siblings in front of me.

"Aspen is missing," I said, trying to hold the tears back.

"He's still not back?" Blue asked.

I shook my head. "I haven't seen him since he left my room the night you found me."

"I didn't see him when I left either." Blue frowned.

"Did you just say that you were in her room?" Poppy asked.

Blue nodded. "Yes, Poppy."

"Blue, if the other Tree Leaders found out about this, I don't know what they'd do," Poppy said, biting her lip.

"Poppy, this is a whole lot bigger than them. This is a lot bigger than anything we have seen before."

"What are you on about?" Poppy looked from me to Blue. "Tell me."

I raised my head to look at Blue, my eyes meeting his. He nodded. "We can trust her."

"Okay."

"Poppy, what I am about to tell you is a secret, and you must keep it to yourself." She nodded. "I mean it."

"Okay, Blue. I get it."

"Willow has Awakened with all four elemental abilities," Blue said. I looked at Poppy for her reaction.

"That's impossible." Poppy chuckled.

"Not impossible," I said quietly. I looked at Poppy to find that she was staring back at me. I felt as if she were reading my mind, trying to figure out whether we were telling the truth or not.

"Prove it." Poppy said.

"Poppy. Don't ask her to do that." Blue said.

"No, it's fine," I said. "I just don't know how I can show you. I don't know how to use the other abilities, they just happen."

"I was thinking about that actually," Blue said. "Now that you've Awakened, you should have some sort of control over your abilities. You should be able to conjure them at will. They may not work how you want them to yet, but they should work."

"How do I do that?" I asked.

"Well, when we want to use our abilities," he said indicating Poppy and himself. "We just concentrate on what we want to do."

"Okay." I concentrated hard on a leaf sitting in front of me, I willed it to float in the air, like Poppy was doing earlier. I closed my eyes to try and concentrate better.

"Whoa," Blue exclaimed. I opened my eyes to find not just that leaf, but all of them in front of me spinning wildly as if they were inside a hurricane. I opened my mouth in surprise. "Now try fire," Blue said, and he and Poppy scrambled backwards slightly.

I closed my eyes, a fire was easy, I thought. I could feel the flames around me before I saw them. I heard Poppy gasp. I opened my eyes and clicked my fingers extinguishing the flames.

"They were purple!" Poppy shouted, pointing. Blue grabbed at her arm.

"Poppy, be quiet." He hissed.

"Sorry," she said quietly. "That was amazing, Willow."

"Water now, come on Willow."

I kept my eyes open this time and cupped my hands out in front of me. It only took a second before I saw the water rising in my hands. I could stop it this time before it overflowed. I pulled my hands apart and the water fell to the ground, turning into ice before it did so. Poppy and Blue stared in astonishment at the ice on the ground. They both seemed too shocked to say anything.

"Earth now Willow. You can do this." Blue said encouragingly.

This was the one ability that I had no clue as to what I was doing. I hadn't even realised that I had conjured up the flowers back home and I had no idea how to do it now. Nevertheless, I closed my eyes and thought of flowers. I shook my head.

"I don't know how to do this one, Blue. I'm sorry." I apologised.

"Willow, open your eyes."

I did as Blue said and was shocked to see that many flowers were now surrounding all three of us.

"Did I do that?" I asked.

"You did," Poppy said, impressed. "This is amazing, how is this even possible?" Poppy asked. I shrugged my shoulders. It was nice that I could share my abilities with somebody else and now that Poppy knew, I was determined to tell Aspen just as soon as I found him.

"Do you believe us now?" Blue said to Poppy.

She shook her head and chuckled. "I believe you, I do. I saw it with my own eyes, but do you know what? I still cannot believe it." She said incredulously.

Blue laughed when Poppy began chuckling once again and then I found myself joining in. I couldn't remember the last time I had laughed, and it felt good. That was until I remembered that there were four people I cared about very much still missing, and I was the only one that could find them.

"Blue, I need to go back to the outside border. I just know, deep down, that all the answers are there." I said.

"I agree. Let's go," he said, standing up.

"What? Now?"

"There's no time like the present," he said, so Poppy and I got up too. "Lead the way."

"Where's the border?" Poppy asked.

"It's situated on the outskirts of Ignis and Ventus."

As we made our way through the forest, I filled them in on the dream that I had experienced during the night.

"Do you think it was like astral-projection?" Poppy asked.

I looked at her with a confused expression on my face.

"Poppy is very interested in witch magic," Blue explained.

"So, what is astral-projection?" I asked.

"Well, it's sort of like you are in two places at once, it usually happens when your sleeping since your mind is in a relaxed state." Poppy explained.

"Do you think that's possible?"

She thought for a moment. "I'd like to believe that it is, and after everything I have experienced today, I think I'm more of a believer than ever."

We carried on walking in silence. I kept thinking about the dream and how real it seemed, and the fact that I was hurt. Could Poppy be right?

A short while later, we walked out into the clearing and I felt the pull of the power radiating from the area. The pull was stronger than before, and I almost felt like this is where I belonged.

"Do you feel it?" I asked the others.

"Feel what?" Blue asked.

"The magic, I can feel it pulsing through me. Are you sure you can't feel it?"

Blue and Poppy shook their heads. I knew that they were telling the truth. I had an inkling that I would be the only one that would be able to feel anything in this clearing.

"Watch this," I said.

I had to show them what would happen when I touched Hazel's resting place. I walked over to the patch of land that was pulsing in front of my eyes. Even now, even after everything, I still found the sight of it mesmerising. It was so curiously inviting, and I longed to touch it again. I knelt on the ground and reached out a hand. My fingertip lightly touched the warm grass and as it did so, that great white light exploded around me.

It was different this time though, I could almost see through the light. Where it was blinding before, I could stand it this time and what I could see through the light shocked me. I thought I could see a person, a woman to be more specific, and she was smiling.

CHAPTER TWENTY
BLUE

As we watched Willow touch the ground around Hazel's resting place, a bright white light emerged from the ground. Slowly, it got bigger and bigger until it was surrounding Willow. It continued to get brighter before bursting outwards, knocking me off my feet.

The light disappeared as quick as it had come, and I noticed that I had been thrown backwards about fifty feet. To my right, Poppy was picking herself up off the ground.

"Are you alright?" I asked. I stood up, dusting the mud and leaves off my shirt.

"I think so," Poppy answered. "What was that?"

"I don't know," I looked around. "We need to go and find Willow. Come on." Poppy and I began running back towards the clearing. When we got there, it was evident that Willow was not.

"Willow!" I shouted. I listened hard for any sign of movement, but it had gone quiet. The birds had even gone silent. "Willow!" I shouted again, but something inside of me knew that she wasn't there.

"Blue, where is she?"

"I don't know."

CHAPTER TWENTY-ONE
WILLOW

I knew I was in the Endarkened as soon as I had opened my eyes and looked around me. The stories my parents had told me about the place was spot on. The Endarkened was a cruel place that twisted your thoughts and emotions until you didn't know who you were anymore. I didn't know how I had got there and I couldn't see Blue or Poppy anywhere.

I had heard of people entering the Endarkened and never returning. Rescues had been made in the past, but when it was realised that those people were no longer themselves, but a more savage version of themselves, it was determined that they couldn't be saved and were left there.

People have stayed away for fear of being trapped in the Endarkened. Once your thoughts turn sinister, it is almost impossible for a person to leave. It is not like they are trapped there, more like that are staying there out of loyalty, but from what I understood growing up, enchantments surrounded the place to keep them from leaving.

I screamed as a pile of leaves in front of me rose from the ground and began to swirl. I knew what was going to happen, but I was frozen in place.

The boy that now stood in front of me looked no older than fifteen and I noticed his eyes first. They were white and the skin on his face was almost the same colour except for the blood-red veins protruding under his skin. He looked angry and it was at the point when his eyes started to bulge out of their sockets that my legs started to work again.

I turned and ran. I didn't know where I was going or what I was going to do, all I knew was that I had to get away from the boy with the white eyes. I kept running, all the while looking behind me sporadically, convinced that the boy was following me.

Trees were scattered to the left and right, and I came to a halt at the edge of a cliff. Leaning forward, the embers of the fiery cavern below made me cough and splutter. The soulless bodies were getting nearer, but there was nowhere else to run. I looked again at the huge split in the ground, sizing up my options.

Looking behind, my heart seemed to stop for a second as the whiter eyes pierced through the darkness. They were too near, their stench filling my nostrils.

I didn't think. I jumped.

I landed, barely, on the other side of the cavern. The trees loomed over me, sheltering me from the flames that licked the ground from below. Surprisingly, they hadn't caught when I had jumped.

I sat back for a while, catching my breath. As I peered through the trees, I could see the whiter eyes standing near the edge looking down. From what I had heard, they were not very bright, but what they had lost in smartness, they made up for in strength. They also had a very strong sense of smell. I certainly didn't want their hands on me.

Moving on, I jumped over a sizeable boulder blocking my way and as I did, I was hoisted into the air harshly. The breath was knocked out of me momentarily and I let out a small whimper. I didn't want any whiter eyes finding me. I tried to use my air abilities to carry myself back down to the ground, but it wasn't working. I tried to conjure up a fire around myself to overpower the ability that was possessing me. Miraculously, it worked, and I found myself falling to the ground.

I picked myself up, the fire still surrounding me, and turned to run again. The fire was protecting me because as I ran, I saw whiter eyes watching me through the trees. The fire lit the way so that I could see where I was going. They backed away from the fire, I noticed, but I wasn't sure how long I could keep it up for. The energy was seeping from my body bit by bit.

I could feel the flames fizzling out until they disappeared completely. I tried to use my other abilities to aid myself, but with no energy, I couldn't conjure anything.

My hands were shaking and the longer I stayed in the Endarkened, the more afraid I became.

I must have stayed still for a moment too long as I was suddenly grabbed from behind. I spun around to face my attacker. I stopped short.

It was as if I was looking at Aspen's face, but it was different. This man was taller and thinner. His nose was identical to my brothers, and despite the white eyes, I could tell that those were the same too. The sharpness of his face and his jawbone were different. This wasn't Aspen. I held on to his arms, keeping him pushed back.

This soulless body was familiar to me in some way. I had known him, I think before his soul was taken.

Suddenly, I was enveloped in complete blackness. I stopped moving, unable to see anything around me. Only the feel of the whiter eye's bony arms beneath my palms kept me grounded. It had also become eerily quiet and I could feel my heart pumping; it almost felt like it was going to burst right out of my chest.

A putrid smell overcame me. I had to fight the urge to be sick. It smelt like rotting fish and eggs. Just when I thought that I could no longer withstand it, there was a huge bolt of lightning that lit up the entire area around me and the smell suddenly felt very unimportant.

I seemed to stop breathing as I tried to comprehend what was happening. It was dark once again, but I couldn't un-see what I had just seen.

Whiter eyes were surrounding me and the soulless man from every direction. Even with the glance from the lightning, there was no denying their cold, soulless eyes leering down at me.

I could feel their bodies towering over me. I could feel their breath on my face, and the smell of their dirty, rotting flesh invading my senses.

I was on the floor now I had let go of the man in front of me, my knees sinking into the wet mud. The bodies around me were closing in and I was struggling to breathe. I put my arms over my head and prayed silently. They were touching me now, their long fingernail claws digging deep into my bare arms. I fought the urge to scream. They were piling on top of me. I couldn't move. I couldn't breathe. Through a small gap of limbs, I could just make out that familiar man standing and just watching.

Complete darkness.

***

"Willow! What happened?" I could hear Blue calling out to me. I felt different now, I could feel a breeze on my arms and I could smell the autumn leaves that I seemed to be crouched upon.

"Willow, Willow, it's me."

I slowly lifted my head to discover Blues concerned eyes. He looked as terrified as I felt. I was suddenly aware of how I must look with tear-stained cheeks and I was covered in mud. I must smell too, I thought. I couldn't get the rotted smell out of my senses.

Seeing Blue looking at me the way he was made me break down. I started sobbing. I was a complete mess, and before I knew it, Blue was pulling me into his arms. I tried to push him away, but he wouldn't let me go. I gave in and leant into him and he tightened his arms around me.

"I'll leave you to it," I heard Poppy say. "I'll meet you at home." I felt Blue nod and I heard her walking away.

"You are okay," Blue said softly. "You're safe." It was comforting, I thought, being close to him. I felt safe. I could feel myself calming down.

I pulled away from Blue and sat beside him, looking down at the ground. I was ashamed to look at him.

"Willow, what happened?" Blue said quietly.

"I don't know," I could barely get the words out. "It must have been another vision. It's just, it felt so real."

"Willow, I don't think it was a vision."

"Why do you say that?"

"Probably because you completely vanished from sight. Also, have you seen your arms? They are a mess, Willow. I'm worried." Blue took my hand in his and squeezed. I looked up at him. He seemed scared.

"What's wrong?" I asked.

Blue chuckled, the light shining in his eyes for a moment.

"What's so funny?" I asked.

"You look like you've been through hell and you're worried about me."

"Oh, is that weird?" I asked. I didn't think it was, but him laughing at me made me doubt myself.

"No, not weird. It just shows me what kind of person you are." Blue answered.

"A good person, I hope?" I said. Blue didn't answer me but instead squeezed my hand once more. I could feel the warmth radiating through my body.

"So, where did you go?" Blue asked. I looked at him and took a deep breath. I didn't how he would react. "Willow?"

"The Endarkened," I said quietly. Blue went quiet for a moment.

"Did you just say…"

"Yep."

"Wow, okay. Do you have any idea how you got there, or how you got out?" Blue asked. I shook my head.

"The bodies were surrounding me while I was on the ground. I couldn't breathe. I thought I was going to die." Blue squeezed my hand again. He still looked so worried. "Then I ended up back here. I don't know how." I explained.

"You are here now. That is all that matters." Blue said. I sniffed, nodding my head.

"Can we get out of here now, please?" I asked.

Blue got up off the ground, pulling me with him. As he did so it was as if his focus shifted, and for a moment I thought he was going to fall over.

"What's wrong?"

"Nothing," Blue said quickly. He had composed himself almost immediately, but his face was pale.

"Tell me," I urged.

Blue shifted uncomfortably and took a deep breath. "I saw it all."

"Saw what?" I asked.

"The Endarkened. I saw you running in the darkness and hovering in the air then falling to the ground. I could feel how scared you were when the whiter eyes were surrounding you."

"How did you see that?" I gasped.

"I don't know Willow, but I am so sorry that you had to go through that alone. If I could take your place, I would."

"I know that Blue, what I am more concerned about is how you could have possibly seen what happened in that horrible place," I said.

"I don't know, it was like I saw it in my head. It happened as I pulled you up from the ground. Maybe you sent me the images?" he sounded confused.

"That is ridiculous," I said.

"Really?" he chuckled. "After everything that has happened, you think that this is ridiculous?"

"I'm glad you think all this is funny," I replied.

"Sometimes you have to laugh at the bad stuff or it will take over." Blue shrugged.

As he took my hand again, I didn't mention how unbelievably vulnerable I had felt when he had seen what he had seen. It wasn't something that I felt comfortable mentioning. Not until I was sure.

"Willow, who was that man?" he asked.

"What man?" I knew exactly what man Blue was talking about, but I wasn't sure that I wanted to know the answer yet.

"It doesn't matter," he replied, and just like that he let it go.

I couldn't help thinking that he had seen more than what he said he saw. He kept a hold of my hand as we began walking back towards Ignis.

We had been walking for a while when Blue spoke again. "Willow, did you turn off the trigger system?"

I looked at him for a second. "Maybe," I said. Blue didn't say a word, but there was a hint of a smile on his lips.

CHAPTER TWENTY-TWO
BLUE

As we were walking back towards Ignis through Crownfire, I felt a rumbling beneath us. The rocky ground was shaking, and I knew instantly what was coming.

"Willow, you need to hover," I said as I kicked up from the ground.

"I don't know how," she shouted up to me. I held out my hand, urging her to take hold, but the earthquake was getting stronger.

I was still hovering mid-air as the earthquake hit, unable to make it to the ground to help Willow. I could barely feel the tremors at all, but the vibrations from the seismic activity were running through my body.

"You have to concentrate!" I shouted through the noise. I could see Willow knelt on the ground in front of me. She had her head in her hands and she was screaming.

Suddenly, it dawned on me that she was in pain; I thought that she was just scared. She was extra sensitive and susceptible to the elements, so it was obvious that the earthquake would affect her mentally.

I lowered myself down to the ground and rushed over to her. I covered her body, shielding her from the falling tree branches.

"What are you doing?" Willow yelled. "Go back, where it's safe." Willow tried to push me off her, but she seemed too weak.

"Just keep your head down!" I yelled back at her. Willow gave up the fight and crouched down further. I pressed my body closer to her.

"Blue, it hurts," Willow shouted, her voice muffled beneath me.

"I know," I said. "It will be over soon." I could feel her body shaking beneath me.

It had only been minutes, but it had felt much longer. Willow stopped shaking and I could feel the earth begin to calm down.

Slowly, we got up and Willow lifted her head. I tried to stand, but when I did, I stumbled back to the ground.

"Are you okay?" Willow ran over to me. "What happened?"

I shook my head. "Just give me a minute," I replied weakly and shakily. I took a few deep breaths, and I could feel the colour appearing on my cheeks.

CHAPTER TWENTY-THREE
WILLOW

I had felt his energy pouring into me when his body had surrounded me. I didn't know how I had managed to do it because I wasn't trying to do anything.

How was I going to tell Blue that I had made him weak, especially when he had risked his life to save mine? I couldn't get my head around it.

I looked back over at him, sitting on the ground. He still looked tired and he had very dark circles around his eyes, which suddenly opened wide, his face becoming serious.

"What is it?" I asked.

"The Tree Council are calling a meeting. We have to go."

"How do you know that?" I asked again.

"Willow, we must go, but they cannot see us together."

Blue held out his hand for me to take, which I do, but he is weak and unsteady. I moved his arm over my shoulder to hold his weight better.

"What are you doing?" he asked, pulling his arm away from me.

"I'm trying to help you."

"I am fine."

"Will you stop being so stubborn and let me help you?" Blue looked about ready to collapse. "We can't stay here, you said that yourself."

"Fine," he said in defeat and he reluctantly put his arm over my shoulder.

As we started to move I realised that it would take a lot longer than I expected. I couldn't bear his weight any more than he could. The concentration on his face though was astonishing. He was trying so hard to keep his weight off me.

"We need to stop," I said.

"No, we must keep going." He urged.

"Blue, you need a minute to get your breath back."

I stopped, knowing that he couldn't walk without me. I helped him to slowly lower himself to the ground, and then I looked around to check that we were still alone before I sat down beside him. He was lying down now, his eyes closed.

"Blue?"

"Yeah?"

I picked a blade of grass and twirled it between my fingers. I didn't know how to say it. "I'm sorry," I said quietly.

"What for?" he asked, opening his eyes. He shielded them from the sun with his hand.

"I think that I did this to you."

"What do you mean?" he asked.

"I think I'm the one that drained you of your energy."

Blue sat up slowly and looked at me. I quickly looked down at my hands. "Willow, that is impossible. Don't be silly."

"I felt it, Blue. I felt myself getting stronger. You got weaker. What other explanation is there?" I said. I chanced a look at him. He was staring right back at me.

"Willow, if by some chance you did do it, and I mean that it would be the tiniest chance ever, you didn't mean it."

"Maybe you should just go on without me. It will be safer anyway." I said.

"Willow, wouldn't you rather just figure this out? You can't just keep running away." He said. I looked at Blue, his expression was fierce. Angry. I turned away, this wasn't the Blue that I was used to.

"You don't understand what it's like," I said quietly. I could feel the tears starting to burn at the corners of my eyes.

"Tell me. Don't shut me out, Willow. I'm not going anywhere."

His voice was softer now, the Blue that I knew. I looked up, his eyes were soft. He reached over to tuck a strand of my hair behind my ear. The feeling that somebody was there for me was empowering. I let my emotions take over momentarily as our eyes locked. It was as if nothing else mattered and there was nobody else in the world. It was only when the ground moved again that I came back to reality as a sharp pain occurred behind my eyes.

"It's okay. It's just an aftershock." Blue said.

The tremor only lasted for a few seconds in which time Blue had taken my hand again. His hands were freezing.

"Are you okay?" I asked.

"Yes, I'm fine."

"No, you're not. Your freezing." I said.

"It is most likely from the lack of energy or something."

"Maybe, or maybe you're in shock. Hold still for a minute." I said. I took both of his hands and closed my eyes.

"What are you doing?" he asked astonished.

"Will you just be still and quiet please."

I focused on the warmth flowing through my body. My heart quickened as I could feel the fire inside me. I concentrated on radiating the heat through my fingers and when I heard Blue gasp, I knew that it had worked. I opened my eyes to see Blue's reaction.

"How are you doing that?" he exclaimed.

"Fires my thing, remember?"

"I know, but you couldn't control it before," he said. "I'm warm enough now, by the way."

"It's a strange feeling," I explained. "I just feel like the elemental abilities inside me are getting stronger. I'm not sure how I did that just now, I just did it."

"That's amazing, do you realise the things you could do?"

"Yes, I do, which is why nobody must ever know. It's not normal, Blue."

"I know. Nobody will hear it from me, I promise."

I searched his eyes to see if he was telling the truth. People always seemed to trust me, but I struggled to trust them back.

CHAPTER TWENTY-FOUR
BLUE

"Willow, we need to go. Now." I said, holding my head.

"Why?"

"The Tree Council are waiting for us. Oakley is mad." I explained.

"How do you know that?" Willow asked again.

"It's hard to explain," I said. "It's like a signal pounding through my head. I can hear Oakley's voice echoing through my mind, demanding to know where we are." The pain was now affecting my vision.

"Why can't I feel it?" Willow asked. "I'm on the council too."

"They're calling for you too. They believe that you are receiving the signal. I have no idea why you're not."

"Strange," she said. "We better get going then."

"Yes, we should. We cannot arrive together though." I repeated straightening up, the pain had finally subsided a little.

"Are you going to be able to walk on your own?"

"I will be fine," I said, giving her a small smile. Willow looked as if she didn't believe me, but didn't argue. "I will see you there." Willow nodded and walked back the way we had come.

I watched her go and then sat down on a nearby tree trunk; a victim of the tremors.

My legs felt like dead weights beneath me, and I felt like I hadn't eaten for a week. The pain intensified again, and I knew that I must move if only to stop myself from lying down.

I tried to teleport instead, but I didn't have the energy to make a small breeze, let alone a tornado.

As I made my way through the debris-laden paths, Oakley's voice screamed through my head again. The loudness stopped me in my tracks, but I could see Crownfire ahead of me.

I finally made it to the Ventus platform and I let out a sigh of relief as it lifted me to the Council and I took my place next to my sister.

"Where have you been?" Oakley boomed. I found it hard to catch my breath, so I just shook my head instead.

CHAPTER TWENTY-FIVE
WILLOW

I couldn't stand still, I was anxiously awaiting Blues arrival, and as soon as I saw his platform rising, I seemed to stop breathing. When he finally stood next to Poppy, I could feel my body relax. He was okay. He looked exhausted, but he was okay.

I hadn't realised how much I cared about him until I had to leave him in the forest. I had almost turned back several times on the way to Crownfire.

Oakley was demanding to know where he'd been, but Blue was too tired to reply. His sister was worried about him, I could see it in her face. His eyes were bright, despite his weakened body. I felt like he was studying me. Could he be worried about me? No, he couldn't possibly be. He couldn't be worried about somebody that had weakened him the way I had.

I let the thoughts leave my head and listened into the Council. Oakley had abandoned his interrogation of Blue, at least for now, and he had moved on to the earthquake.

"I don't think that the earthquake that we experienced earlier was natural. I think it was made deliberately." Oakley droned on.

Gasps accompanied the accusation of course. The thought that somebody would cause those tremors on purpose was hard to digest. It was also unheard of.

"Don't you think that it may have been an accident?" Lily asked. There was a bit of murmuring to this question.

"It's happened before," Poppy added. "Especially if someone is coming into their abilities."

"You would say that, wouldn't you? Those in Ventus seem to let their abilities waver all the time." Oakley snapped.

"Excuse me Oakley, but you cannot point the finger when you have no proof," Blue spoke up. He had finally found his voice, although Oakley snapping at his sister might have had something to do with it.

"You need to watch who you are speaking to, boy. I haven't finished with you yet." Oakley snarled

"Well, unless it happens again, I think that you need to accept that this was an accident," Blue said. Amazingly, Oakley looked angrier than ever, but he didn't say a word.

I looked around at the other Tree Leaders, they all seemed to agree with Blue.

"Willow?" I lifted my head to see who had spoken. It was Dune. "Where is your brother?" he asked.

"I don't know," I murmured.

"Speak up, girl," Oakley chimed in.

"I said, I don't know," I repeated.

"Well, there will be consequences for his lack of attending." Oakley snarled.

"You don't understand…"

"Don't tell me what I understand and what I don't." Oakley boomed. Red flames erupted around us.

"Oakley, calm down," Dune said. I looked over at Blue, but I could tell he was barely listening. He looked as if he was about to faint. "Willow, please explain."

"I haven't seen him since my birthday. I feel like something is wrong." Dune looked as if he was thinking.

"Willow, please let me know if he is not back by the week's end. There is no need to call a meeting. You can send word through the fire like your parents used to."

"I don't know how to do that," I explained.

"You have awakened now, yes?" I nodded. "Then you will know what to do."

"Dismissed." Oakley roared.

When my platform landed on the ground, I walked over to the large tree where Blue and I usually met. I waited until Poppy rounded the corner. She was holding Blue up for support. I ran towards them.

"What happened to him?" Poppy asked, clearly annoyed and worried.

"I don't know. I felt like I might have drained his energy when he was protecting me from the earthquake. I had this weird feeling and then when we got up, Blue was weakened."

"Willow, it's not your fault." Blue gasped, bending over.

"I think I should get him home." Poppy said. "He probably just needs some rest, time to recuperate."

I was left alone as I watched Poppy teleport them both away. I made my way home, feeling guiltier that I had in my entire life.

CHAPTER TWENTY-SIX
BLUE

The following morning, I strolled through the forest next to Ignis after teleporting to the outskirts. The fact that Willow had turned off the trigger system was certainly advantageous. The closer I walked to her neighbouring community, the more I could sense her. It was strange. I had never felt anything like it before. It was a good feeling, if not a little weird. It was almost like I could find her in a crowd of a thousand people. It was like we had an invisible tether attached to us, only I didn't know if she felt the same.

As I got closer to her house, there was a fire burning in the pit outside. Willow was sat next to it; her eyes were closed. I was almost upon her when she spun around. A smile lit up her face.

"You're okay," she squealed as she ran over to me. She flung her arms around my neck, giving me the tightest hug ever.

"I told you I was okay, didn't I," I said as she pulled away.

"You did. I didn't believe you though." She said as she sat back down next to the fire. I followed suit, sitting down next to her.

"It's a bit early for fire, isn't it?" I said, indicating the flames in front of us.

"Oh, I made it last night," Willow said.

"Have you been out here all night?" I asked. Looking at her now though, I could tell that she had. There were dark circles around her eyes and she looked pale. Tired.

"I couldn't sleep," she shrugged.

"Dreams again?" I asked. I was worried. "You need to sleep, Willow. Keep your strength up." I added.

She shook her head. "No dreams. I just felt guilty. I've been trying to come up with ways that I could have done that to you, and ways that I could fix it."

I looked over at her. "Willow, please don't beat yourself up over it. It was nothing. Really. I'm fine now." She looked at me, hurt clouding her eyes. "Listen to me," I said. "I. Am. Fine. Please believe that."

"I do believe it, but for a while, you weren't and that was all my fault. It's never going to happen again." She got up off the log and walked over to the house. I followed her. She had to get over her guilt, or she wasn't going to be of any use to anyone.

"Willow, can I come in?" I asked as she walked into her house. She hadn't closed the door entirely, but I wasn't in the habit of going in uninvited. She appeared at the threshold and threw the door open completely. I walked inside. It looked like a bomb had hit the place.

"What happened?" I exclaimed. Looking around, I noted the table and chairs upended. Smashed plates on the floor and the sink overflowing with dishes.

"I got a bit angry last night," Willow said, shrugging. I was concerned, but I didn't know what to say. Instead, I grabbed her hand.

"Come on," I said, pulling her back outside.

"Come on where Blue? I really can't be bothered."

"Let's go flying, see if we can see anything from above," I said.

Willow seemed to be considering the idea. Finally, she nodded her head and followed me outside. I led her to a clearing just before the thick of trees, but far enough away from the community. From here, we could see the Youngers of Ignis in the training ring.

I closed my eyes to conjure a Sylph when Willow put her hand on my arm.

"I'll do it," she said. "You're not strong enough yet." I nodded my head in response, even though I felt fine.

I watched as she closed her eyes. Momentarily, her face became very pale as she used all her energy conjuring a bird. There was a short pause before I saw anything materialising.

"Erm, Willow? Open your eyes." She did as I said, and I saw her look at the creature in awe.

"What is that?" she asked, walking around the creature.

Its wings were barely visible, almost see-through and it had hooves for feet. It clawed the ground impatiently, staring at us with black, beady eyes. The rest of its body was white, apart from the head, which was jet black.

"That would be a Boobrie," I said.

"Really? It's different from how I thought it would look," she said.

"How are you so calm?" I asked her. She didn't look panicked or scared. She almost seemed as if she was intrigued.

"Why wouldn't I be calm?" she answered. "Come on, let's go." She reached up to touch the Boobrie.

"Willow, we can't fly on that creature," I said, shocked.

"Why not?"

"The reason we cannot fly that bird is that if anybody sees a fire user and an air user flying on the back of a bird associated with water and ice, I can't even begin to imagine what people would say," I explained.

Willow seemed to think for a moment before answering. "I guess you're right," she replied. "How are we going to fly then?"

The Boobrie melted into a puddle of water around our feet. I closed my eyes and thought of the Sylph. I opened them to find the familiar creature flapping its wings waiting for its riders.

"Let's go," I said as I jumped on to its back. I held my hand out for Willow and she took it without hesitation. I pulled her up behind me and she put her arms around my waist. For a moment, I was frozen. I didn't want to risk her moving and the warm feeling to go away.

"Blue?" she prompted. I took a deep breath as I steered the Sylph upwards. The ground left us as we soared higher into the sky. I drove the creature over towards the outside border.

"Keep your eyes open, Willow. Let me know if you see anything unusual."

"Okay." I continued to look down as well, but so far all I could see were trees. They dominated most of the area, shielding all houses, the school and training ground from view. "Blue?" Willow said.

"Yeah?"

"Thanks for this," she said.

"No problem."

Willow squeezed my waist a little harder and I felt her head rest against my back. For a minute, I forgot our mission and I was comforted in the fact that I was in good company.

"Blue, what is that?" Willow brought me out of my momentary dream state.

"What is what?" I asked, confused. She tapped my shoulder as she pointed down to the ground. I followed her gaze, having to look twice. I couldn't quite comprehend what I could see. "I have no idea."

I began to guide the Sylph down towards the ground and as we glided closer, it suddenly became clear what we were seeing.

We could no longer see the trees; the ground was covered in a thick grey fog. The fog was moving slowly, like clouds moving across the sky. We watched as the fog made its way towards the Ignis border. I rose the Sylph higher and noticed the same thing on the border of Glacies and Terra. It was slowly making its way through the Zones. Rising higher, we could see the path that the fog was leaving behind. It looked like snow.

"What the hell, Blue?" Willow said as she took in the scene before us. I had never seen anything like it. Snow and ice never left the Glacies Zone and the fog was an almost impossible occurrence in all other Zones.

"We need to tell someone about this," I said.

"Who?" Willow asked.

"I'm going to message Dune. He can make sure Oakley finds out. I have not got the patience to deal with him right now." I said. Willow nodded.

"I don't think we are going to find anything up here, Blue. It's hard to see anything anyway, what with the fog and the trees." Willow said.

"I agree. Come on, my energy is draining anyway. I need to land this bird."

I turned the Sylph around and headed back towards Ignis. I needed to drop Willow off and I knew exactly who I needed to speak to.

As we landed, the Sylph disappeared in a twister. A huge gust of air erupted from the creature and knocked Willow off her feet. She stumbled backwards falling to the ground. I ran over, helping her to her feet.

"Sorry, I should have warned you about that," I apologised.

"It's no problem," Willow said, and for once she had a smile on her face. "Even though we didn't find out anything about the disappearances, I'm glad we did that. It was fun. I've missed that."

"Well then, I'm glad I was able to put a smile on your face. It suits you Willow."

CHAPTER TWENTY-SEVEN
BLUE

I could sense the magic as soon as I walked onto Ventus territory. I listened through the wind and smiled as I could hear the chorus of applause at the top of the mountain. I knew that would be where my sister was, so I teleported straight to the top.

I stumbled as I landed.

"You really should be better at that by now," Poppy said walking over to me.

"That wasn't my fault," I said. "There was a particularly large breeze just as I landed."

"Sure," she said.

"Blue!" I turned to see Aviv running towards me. Aviv was only thirteen, but his abilities were progressing faster than most at his age. He was tall and his gangly frame made him seem older than he was. His black hair was cut short, showing off his high cheekbones.

In Ventus, Youngers at this age could just about produce a breeze if their abilities had begun to show. Aerokinesis was the first thing that they learnt.

"Watch this," he said. I stood back and watched as Aviv began to produce a mini twister in front of our eyes. Leaves and dirt from the ground were swept up in its path. Aviv managed to keep it up for a couple of minutes before it dissipated.

"Wow, that's great," I exclaimed. Aviv grinned at me with pride. I looked around the training ground at the other Youngers, some as young as ten, watching with admiration.

I used to watch my parents train when I was younger and it was astonishing how much I learnt. When I was made Tree Leader, I insisted that the Youngers go to the training ground too, whether their abilities had begun showing or not.

"You're doing a great job with them," I said to Poppy.

"Thank you, brother," she said, looking around at her students. "So, you didn't come up here to oversee the training. What do you want, Blue?" she asked.

I was watching Aviv twirling leaves around. His sister, Clover, was standing just a short distance away watching her brother with an intent look on her face. Clover was a year older and hadn't made much progress with her abilities. I had reassured her many times that everybody progresses at different rates. It hadn't stopped her from feeling jealous.

"Blue?"

"Huh? Oh, sorry Poppy. What did you say?" I asked.

"Where were you just now?" she asked.

"I was just thinking about Clover. Is she showing any signs of her abilities yet?"

"She is. It is a slow progression, but it's coming along." Poppy said watching the siblings. "Having a brother who is so much more advanced doesn't help." She added.

I nodded. "I'm sure it doesn't," I said. "How do you feel about having such an advanced big brother?" I grinned at her.

"I wouldn't know how that feels," Poppy said.

"Sure, you don't," I replied with a smirk. "How much longer is training, Poppy? I could use your help with something." I said.

"We are just about done. I'll send everyone back to the school for theory and then we can go back to the house."

"No problem."

I hung back as my sister began to stop the training. The Youngers made their way back down the mountain, waving to me as they did.

A good relationship with the community was what I had always wanted as a Tree Leader. The Tree Leaders had always felt intimidating to me when I was growing up, even my parents, and I never felt that I could talk freely to any of them.

It was different now, in Ventus anyway.

***

A short while later, Poppy and I were sat in our living area.

"So, what's up?" Poppy asked.

"Well, Willow and I saw something strange today around Glacies whilst we were flying."

"What kind of strange?" she asked. Surprisingly, she didn't mention the fact that I was with Willow alone. Again.

"Fog."

"What's so weird about that?" she asked. "Glacies is almost always surrounded by fog," she said.

"It was travelling towards Ignis and Terra. It was leaving a trail of snow."

Poppy looked thoughtful for a moment. A breeze came through the large opened window blowing the flowers on the small table between us. I got a sudden aroma of sweet fragrant lavender.

"It could be an element imbalance. It's not unheard of."

"What do you mean?" I asked.

"Sometimes the elements can become unbalanced. The cause can be several things, such as the weather being too warm or too cold." She explained.

"So, how can we fix it?"

"Usually, an imbalance will right itself. It's happened before. There's no reason to panic." She said.

"What if it doesn't fix itself?" I asked.

"I don't know, Blue. We will just deal with it if it comes, I suppose," she said. "Have you told anyone else about this?"

"I sent a message to Dune to let him know."

Poppy nodded. "That's probably for the best. I don't think that there is much you can do, other than keeping an eye on it."

CHAPTER TWENTY-EIGHT
WILLOW

I was sat in the kitchen wondering about that fog. If it reached Ignis, I didn't know what I would do. Ignis wasn't the right climate for fog and the community wasn't used to the cold.

I walked into Aspen's room. The sheer blueness hit me first. The walls, the bedspread, even the carpet was blue. I don't how he put up with it. It was very tidy. He always used to complain about how my room was such a mess.

The room still smelled of him.

I missed him.

Suddenly, there was ear-piercing scream echoing from outside. I jumped in fright before running through the kitchen and out the back door. A crowd had gathered just inside the forest. A young girl was lying on the ground.

"What happened?" I shouted. As I neared, I recognised the young girl as Fern. She was crying and holding the bottom of her leg. Blood was seeping through her fingers.

"It was a Superno," Acacia explained when I got there.

"What? Are you sure?" I couldn't believe what I was hearing or what I was seeing.

"Olive and I saw it," Acacia said.

"Okay, then we need to get out of the forest. Boys? Can you help Fern over here please?" I watched as Ash and Linden carefully picked Fern up and transported her to the campfire area.

"Is she going to be okay?" Olive asked, her voice was so quiet that she almost squeaked out her question.

I knelt next to Fern and moved her hand out of the way. The wound didn't look too deep, but you could see the jagged edges of her skin from the Superno's razor-sharp teeth.

"Here," Linden said, handing me a large piece of cloth.

"Thank you," I pressed the material against the wound, trying to remember my training from school. We had focused more on burns and only a little on cuts. The bleeding seemed to be slowing. "Was it a Shadow or an Aurora?" I asked.

"It was a Shadow," Acacia said. "I saw its red eyes so clearly in the daylight." She shivered.

The Auroras outranked the Shadows, keeping them in line and making sure that attacks didn't happen.

"Why was it out in the daylight?" Ash asked.

"I don't know," I answered. "I don't feel confident now leaving you Youngers out here unsupervised. It's not safe."

Slowly, I lifted the material from Fern's leg. The bleeding had stopped, the wound had already started to heal. Fern had also stopped crying.

"What are we supposed to do then?" Acacia asked.

"If you are not in school or at the training ground, then you are at home. I don't want anyone out after dark." I explained.

"But, Willow –"

"No buts, Olive. It's for your protection." I said, a little more harshly than I intended. Olive nodded her head and looked down at her feet.

I helped Fern to stand up, and when I was sure that it wasn't going to start bleeding again, I stood up too.

"Okay, I am going to take Fern home. I suggest that you all follow suit. The sun is already setting." The Youngers all did as I had asked, and while Fern continued to hold my hand, we made our way across to the neighbouring community.

***

When I returned home, I did a quick sweep of the surrounding area to make sure there were no Youngers out of their homes. At the same time, I kept an eye out for any Superno, Shadows or Auroras. The area seemed to be clear.

I collapsed straight into bed when I got to my room, but I struggled with sleep. There seemed to be too much information running through my mind.

***

"Willow." My name echoed through the cave-like walls. I couldn't determine where the sound had come from. I looked around, but I could barely see my hand in front of my face. My eyes adjusted slowly to the darkness, but shadows seemed to occupy every nook and cranny.

"Willow." The voice sounded familiar, but I couldn't think of where. I felt my way along the walls towards where I had thought the voice had originated from.

The walls were rocky and jagged, sharp against my hand. It seemed to go on and on, and I thought it was never-ending until I saw a flickering light in the distance. My eyes had adjusted enough now to make out shapes in the darkness.

"Willow," the voice was louder now, and I finally figured out whom it belonged to.

"Mom?" I shouted out. My voice echoed back to me. I waited quietly for a moment, but she didn't answer. "Mom?"

I smelt it first. That familiar, almost comforting aroma. Smoke. I just had enough time to cover my head with my arms before the fire burst through the tunnel. I felt the flames licking my skin. Burning.

I woke up choking. Smoke filled the room and I struggled to take a breath as it filled my lungs. I doused the fire almost immediately, but some of the sheets were still alight.

Panicking, I tried to think about what to do and just before running to the bathroom to get water, I remembered my newfound water abilities. I concentrated hard, thinking the word water and water all over again.

I gasped as I was showered from head to toe. I opened my eyes to find my room covered in water. Everything was dripping wet and the floor was swimming. Smoke rose like steam. I folded my arms in frustration and felt a searing pain, and I looked down to see an ugly burn rising from my wrist almost to my elbow.

What Aspen had feared had happened. I needed to find a way to control my abilities. He would be losing his mind if he were here.

***

"Willow! Willow!" I ran out of the house to the cries of the Youngers outside. It was clear when I left the house what the problem was. Ice was covering the ground in all directions.

"What happened?" I asked. When I had gone to bed the night before, all had been well. I watched as some of the Youngers slipped over as they headed towards my house. Everybody in the surrounding community and those other communities that resided in Ignis seemed to be heading towards me. The crowd was large as I took it all in.

"When we woke up, the ground was covered," Ash explained, his dark, shaggy hair falling over his face.

"How did this happen, Willow?" Acacia asked.

"I'm not too sure," I answered. The whole Zone seemed confused which was understandable. Never in my lifetime had I known the ice and snow to stray from Glacies and I had no idea what to do about it.

"Maybe we could melt It?" Linden offered. I looked around at the small group of Youngers who looked very eager to try out their abilities. They all nodded in response to Linden's solution.

"We could try it," I answered. "Maybe we should all hold hands?"

Everybody gathered around me as I took Linden's hand and then Acacias. The others joined in, including the Youngers not showing signs of their abilities yet. "Olive, come on," I urged to the young girl. She ran over with a huge smile on her face.

"What do we do, Willow?" Ash asked. He was stood opposite me on the far side of the circle.

"Concentrate on what you want to do. We want to warm the ground and melt the ice, but we don't want fire."

The Youngers nodded. I looked around, even the community Elders were out in force. There were more than fifty of us in all. We needed the entire Ignis community if we wanted to succeed.

I closed my eyes concentrating hard on what we needed and then I felt the warmth radiating from my hands. I opened my eyes to see that everybody felt the same. There was an orange glow that now surrounded the circle and slowly, very slowly, the ice and snow began to melt. The familiar red and orange leaves began to once again show through the snow and puddles began to form around everybody's feet.

"Open your eyes," I said. There were gasps all around.

"We did it," Acacia said. I smiled. Others nodded, grins on their faces.

"Willow, I did it. I felt it." Olive exclaimed.

"I told you, you had it in you all along, Olive. It just takes time to surface." Olive looked the happiest I had seen her in a long time. Everybody was clapping and whooping.

CHAPTER TWENTY-NINE
BLUE

I arrived in Ignis just after breakfast. I had an inkling of where we might find some answers and I was keen for Willow to accompany me.

Though it was early, the Ignis Zone was quieter than usual. I looked around at the dead campfires that were usually burning through the night and at the closed doors and windows of the houses surrounding them.

I walked over to Willows door and knocked. I stood back waiting for her to answer. I was about to knock again when the door slowly creaked open.

"Blue? What are you doing here?" Willow asked. She was still in her pyjamas. She looked very pale.

"What's wrong?" I asked.

"Nothing," she replied, although her eyes said a different story. She was avoiding eye contact and I could tell that something was wrong.

"Can I come in?" She looked as if she was considering my question but then stood back for me to enter. We went into the kitchen and Willow went to make some tea.

"Willow. What happened to your arm?" I exclaimed. I had just sat down at the table and when Willow had lifted the pot off the stove, her sleeve had rolled up. I watched as she hastily pulled it back down again.

"It's nothing," she said, as she carried on making the tea.

I watched as she filled two cups, the smell of liquorice overpowering the room. I waited until she was sat down at the table.

"Let me see," I said. When she looked at me, a different Willow that I had come to know was staring back. Her cheekbones stuck out sharply. Her eyes had sunken into her eye sockets. They looked dark like she hadn't slept for days and with her pale face, she looked almost skeletal.

Gingerly, she lifted her sleeve, wincing as she did so. The burn was an angry red. It covered her entire lower arm and was covered in white blisters.

"Have you put something on that?" I asked, concerned.

"Of course, I have," Willow snapped."It's fine."

"Okay, okay," I said holding my hands up in defeat. "Can I at least ask how you did it?"

"It was just a bad dream, that's all," she said.

"A bad dream that made you burn your arm?" I said, finding it increasingly hard to believe her.

"Blue, you don't understand. Sometimes my dreams can be pretty intense." I raised my eyebrows. "Fine. Don't believe me."

"Willow –"

"No Blue, I think it is time you left. I have a lot to do today."

"Willow –"

"Goodbye, Blue."

Willow turned away from me and walked out of the kitchen. I had no choice but to leave. However, as I left, I did notice the pillows and the blankets on the sofa in the living area.

***

I paused as I neared the cave mouth. I was still trying to determine whether it was a good idea to be here alone. My father had told me about the Acalica, or weather fairies as he used to call them. They were private creatures who liked to keep to themselves. I had never seen one. My father had though. He said that they were arrogant little things that were very protective of their personal space.

I stooped to fit through the cave entrance. The top of my head brushed the top of the cave as I crawled through the mouth. However, the cave inside was vast compared to its entrance. I couldn't see the ceiling as it was too high. There was a small fire burning in one corner which provided an orange glow, making the cave feel warm and homely.

On first inspection, it appeared to be empty. Since I didn't know what I was looking for, I took another look around, stepping further inside as I did so.

The crackling of the fire almost drowned out the faint whimper I suddenly heard from the far corner. I squinted, trying to see into the shadows. As I moved closer, I could see a small white creature lying on the ground. It looked to be about two feet in height and it wore nothing but a white scrap of cloth around its middle. The Acalica was shaking violently.

My father had once told me that the Acalica consisted of many different colours depending on the element or weather to which they were accustomed.

The Acalica that lay at my feet was white and seemed to be tied to the Glacies Zone. I knelt on the ground, my knee hard against the stone floor. I reached out my hand to touch the creature, and as I did so, it stopped shaking and opened one of its eyes. It was as black as night and seemed lifeless.

"Fear the necromancer," the Acalica whispered, and as it opened its mouth, small jagged teeth were exposed.

"What do you mean?" I asked. Its eye turned to me before closing again.

"You must stop the spreading," it said. I was about to ask what it meant again when the Acalica went still. I nudged its thin, scaly arm. It was hard to the touch and cold. It was almost like its skin was frozen.

I tried to think back to what my father had said about the Acalica. I was almost sure that they couldn't die, but they could be weakened. They had been around since the Darkest Times, the earliest point in history that had been recorded.

There was nothing I could do for the creature, so I took off my jacket and laid it over the Acalica's tiny body. I left the cave with one last look, making a mental note to come back. There was one thing that I was sure of, and that was that I thought my sister was correct about the unbalancing.

CHAPTER THIRTY
WILLOW

I couldn't believe that I had spoken to Blue like that. He probably thought that I was a spoiled brat.

I was stood in the middle of my room breathing in the smell of burned material and feeling the cold wetness of the floor. I knelt, placing my hand's palm down on the carpet. I closed my eyes. I felt the overheating sensation first, the feeling that my body was boiling and bubbling inside. I felt the heat radiating from my hands and I opened my eyes to find steam erupting all around me.

The carpet was no longer wet and squelchy, but dry and warm. I sighed in relief, glad that one problem was solved. There was nothing I could do about the burnt bed covers or the singed curtains.

I collected my bed things from the sofa and took them back to my room. When I walked back through the kitchen, I could tell immediately that something was different. As I entered, I stopped short, the atmosphere had changed. The room was no longer hot and humid, but cold.

I dropped the blanket and pillow onto my bed and slowly turned in a circle as I carefully surveyed the room, and as I did I was aware of something moving out of the corner of my eye. When I looked closer though, it seemed to disappear.

Darkness invaded my senses, covering the room in a blanket of shadows.

The most vivid images appeared in my mind. My mother and father were lying in the forest covered in blood, brutally murdered. Aspen was just a short distance away. He was crying out for help. Blue was there too, and he was holding his stomach, blood seeping through his fingers. The expression on his face was panicked and full of fear.

The darkness overwhelmed me once more, completely blocking out the images in my mind. It wasn't enough for me to un-see them though.

Suddenly, I was back in my room, although I was sure that I hadn't left. The shadows were reaching out to me and it finally occurred to me what was happening.

The Umbra.

I tried to focus on the positive. I tried to focus on the good in my life and I tried to un-see the terror of which I had just envisaged. However, the Umbra was too overwhelming.

I slid back into the corner against the wall. The cold seeped into me, taking over my entire body as I shook with fear, the images from before flicking through my mind.

The Umbra pulled me deeper into the darkest part of myself, and I could feel the life being sucked out of me.

I couldn't determine the time scale of events. I couldn't think, and when I thought I couldn't take anymore, something shifted. I could feel myself getting a little warmer. Something was pulling me out of the darkness. The warmth began to invade my body, the shadows slowly turning to light. I grasped the light as it brightened, pulling myself from the fear I had succumbed to.

Soon, the panicked emotions in me eased as I felt a familiar presence. I opened my eyes, squinting against the light.

The Umbra was gone.

"Willow?" I jumped as a soft voice spoke. Blue was sitting next to me, his hand covering my own.

"It was you," I said, interlocking my fingers with his. His grasp gave me strength.

"What do you mean?" Blue asked. He looked confused.

"You pulled me out of the darkness."

"I don't know how I did that. When I came in, the Umbra had taken over. I felt your presence in the darkness, and held your hand." Blue explained. "You did everything else."

"You had everything to do with it, Blue. I don't think I would have come back from that place if you hadn't been there." I replied.

"Willow, it shouldn't have got that far. You know that the Umbra feed and multiply on fear."

"I know."

We sat in silence for a while. It felt a little awkward.

"I'm sorry," I said. "I shouldn't have kicked you out before."

"You had every right to ask me to leave Willow. I should have believed you. I'm sorry too." Blue said. I squeezed his hand and leant in against him.

"You were worried," I said. "There is no need to be sorry about that." I could hear his steady heartbeat through his chest and I felt comforted by his casual stroking of my hair.

"What happened in here?" Blue asked.

"Exactly what I told you before," I said. "In the weeks before the Awakening, I often woke up surrounded by fire. Aspen would always wake me before it got too bad."

"Is that normal for someone in Ignis?" Blue asked.

"Well, you know what happened at Crownfire? When I surrounded myself in flames?" Blue nodded. "Well, that happened to Aspen quite a lot while he was awake, but never while he was asleep. I don't know if it is normal or not."

"Now that Aspen is not here, he isn't around to wake you?" Blue realised.

"Exactly," I said. "I just didn't wake up in time last night and the fire got a little out of control." I looked at Blue, who looked as horrified as I thought he would when I imagined telling him what had happened.

"Willow, you can't go on like that," he said.

"I don't think I have much of a choice, Blue."

"We'll figure it out. Together."

CHAPTER THIRTY-ONE
BLUE

"We have had more meetings in one month than we have had in the last year. What is the problem now?" Oakley said. Once again, he was in a bad mood. Honestly, I felt sorry for his wife. Crimson always looked miserable. It's a shame that she was forced to marry someone like Oakley. I would never let that happen in Ventus.

"Your Zone, Oakley," I said.

"What do you mean, boy?" he snarled.

I thought strategically. I had to be careful now. The other Tree Leaders could not know about Willow and I fraternising outside of the Crownfire meetings.

"I was doing some training a few days ago with some of the Youngers. We were flying high over Sationem when I discovered fog. It was spreading past the Glacies border towards the Ignis and Terra border." I explained.

"Don't be preposterous, boy. What a foolish thing to say." Oakley sneered.

"Oakley," Dune chimed in. "Blue informed me of this situation as soon as he was aware of it. I checked it out for myself and I was shocked to see that it was true."

"Well, why is this happening then?" Oakley asked.

"Honestly?" Dune said. "I have no idea."

"Well, if I can propose a theory?" I asked. Everybody turned to look at me. Willow was staring right at me. I hadn't had the chance to tell her about the trip to the caves yet.

"Go on," Dune urged.

"Poppy had an interesting theory, to which she explained an elemental imbalance. I took it upon myself to visit one of the Acalica."

"Blue," Dune interrupted. "This is something that you should have informed to the Council before taking action."

"I know," I said. "But there was no time. I just had to see for myself what was happening." I took a breath waiting for anyone else to start reprimanding me.

"What did you find?" the soft voice of Lily asked.

"Proof. Proof that something is happening. The Acalica was weakened. It was lying on the floor close to death."

"Did it say anything?" Lily asked.

"It did," I said.

"Don't keep us in suspense, boy." Once again, the flames burned red as they always did when Oakley spoke. I always did wonder what he was like away from the meeting. I wondered if he was this angry all the time.

"It said, 'fear the necromancer'."

"What does that even mean?" Oakley said.

"I have no idea," I replied. I looked around at the other Leaders. Nobody seemed particularly concerned.

"It seems that there may be something happening out there," Dune said. "I think that we need to be extra vigilant and report anything that seems strange."

"That's it?" It was Willow that spoke this time. Her face said it all. She looked incredulous. I knew how she felt. The Tree Council were lax in making decisions, often making them too late.

"If this is indeed an unbalancing of the elements, it may right itself on its known without the need for interfering. Interfering may cause more damage in the long run." Dune explained. "I think that the best thing to do is to wait it out unless the occurrences get substantially worse."

"Fine by me," Oakley said. "Now can we please dismiss this meeting. I have better things to do than standing around here discussing something that might not even happen."

"Very well," Dune said. "Dismissed."

***

I waited for Willow after I had ejected from the platform. Poppy was standing by my side. Despite the fact she didn't seem so concerned before, she seemed to have changed her mind and looked a little worried.

"It will be alright, Poppy," I said reassuringly. She smiled.

"I'll leave you to it, Blue. Can you come home soon though? I don't see you much anymore. I'm sure the kids would love it if you taught a class."

"Of course, I will. I won't be long, I promise." I said. She kissed my cheek before turning to teleport back to Ventus.

"Blue?" Willow was stood behind me.

"Hi, Willow. Are you okay?"

"I'm fine. Why didn't you tell me? You shouldn't have gone to see the Acalica on your own. Anything could have happened." She seemed genuinely hurt that I hadn't told her.

"Nothing did happen. I was going to tell you the night the Umbra came, and it just went out of my head. I'm sorry. You have enough to worry about without me dumping stuff on you as well." I said.

"You don't need to worry about me, Blue. I am quite capable of looking after myself." Willow said.

"I know that," I said. "I don't want to worry you unnecessarily Willow. I care about you too much." I admitted. Willow stood looking at me. She looked like she didn't know what to say. "Listen, I have to go, okay?" Willow nodded. "I'll see you later."

CHAPTER THIRTY-TWO
WILLOW

I watched as Blue followed Poppy back to Ventus. He left in a blur as he teleported in front of me. I still hadn't figured out how to do that yet.

I was about to head back to Ignis when something caught my eye. A haze of blue and red hidden behind the trees. I squinted as I tried to distinguish what it was. I walked a little closer. It was a boy.

"Hello," I said. The boy came out from behind the tree he was hiding behind. Or spying behind. "Who are you?" I asked.

"I am Aviv. Nice to meet you." He said, holding out his hand. I shook it.

"Nice to meet you too," I replied.

"What were you talking to Blue about?"

"Oh, you know Blue, do you?" Aviv nodded. "We were just talking about Tree Council stuff," I said hastily. I looked at Aviv a little more closely. He looked familiar to me somehow. I couldn't determine how. It was like I had known him a long time, but I had only just met him.

"Blue is the best," he said. "He teaches me a lot," Aviv explained.

"You're from Ventus then?" I asked. "What is Blue like as a teacher? Strict? Soft?" Aviv laughed.

"You like him, don't you?" Aviv asked.

I looked at him curiously. "I have no idea what you mean. Why do you even care? Shouldn't you be at school or something right now?"

"I should be. I am just curious."

"About what?"

"I am wondering about the pull. The sensation that I have been experiencing for a while now. Today, I decided to follow it. It led me to you," he explained.

"What do you mean?" I asked, and a little uncertain that I wanted to know the answer. This young boy who couldn't be older than fifteen was insinuating that I was his answer to something.

"What I mean is that some type of invisible rope is drawing me to you. I want to know why.

"Well, I can't imagine what that could mean. I don't feel anything." I said.

Aviv shrugged. "I don't know what it means either, but I am going to find out."

He turned and walked away from me. I watched as he rounded the corner and disappeared into the trees. I believed him. Every word. I felt apprehensive about what it all meant though. I had a bad feeling and found myself thinking that I didn't want to know what it was all about at all.

CHAPTER THIRTY-THREE
BLUE

"Have you ever wondered what's beyond?" I asked as we watched the sunrise. Willow's hand was cold in mine despite the fact she had fire running through her veins. It baffled me.

"I'm sorry, what?" she asked.

Distracted wasn't the word I used to describe Willow lately. It was more than that. It was as if she wasn't there half the time.

"I asked if you ever wondered what was beyond?" I repeated, nodding towards the setting sun.

"Oh, you mean the ripple?" she asked. I nodded. "I've thought about it, I suppose. I find it a little scary that there is a whole other world beyond Sationem, especially one that we barely know anything about."

"I understand what you mean, but aren't you a little curious about what's out there?" I asked.

I looked over at Willow after a moments silence. She was back in her little world again, not hearing a word I had said.

After a few minutes, and just as the sunset was at its most spectacular, Willow leaned into me and I put my arm around her. A golden glow shimmered over everything making it look magical.

"This is nice," Willow said.

"What's nice?" I asked. As the sunset and the surroundings grew darker, the atmosphere changed. It was peaceful.

"Being here with you," Willow said. "Forgetting about everything else for a while."

I held her closer. "I know what you mean."

We both sat there for a while, the calmness of dusk overwhelming. Relaxing. It was only when Willow let out a shiver that I realised how long we had been sat there for.

"You know we have to go home soon, right? Poppy will be wondering where I am." I said.

"I know," Willow replied, a sadness in her voice.

"What's wrong?"

"I hate it there, without my parents and Aspen. It's too quiet."

I turned to face her. "I would love nothing more than to stay with you, for however long necessary, but you know it's not that simple. We could both be exiled." I said.

"I know."

"One day things will change, but until then, we have to keep quiet."

"I know," Willow repeated. "Will you come by first thing in the morning?" she asked.

"Of course."

CHAPTER THIRTY-FOUR
WILLOW

I looked around at the empty house.

Quiet.

Too quiet.

I walked to my room and shut the door, at least then I could pretend that the house was full. My parents were asleep in their room next door and Aspen was in the kitchen filling up on food as usual.

I laid my head down on the pillow and closed my eyes.

CHAPTER THIRTY-FIVE
BLUE

When I woke up, it was almost dawn. The sky was beginning to lighten. Something had pulled me out of sleep though and it took me a moment to discover why.

Willow.

I scrambled out of bed, struggling to find my clothes. The floor was covered with junk and I knew that Poppy would go crazy if she saw it. After locating my clothes and getting dressed, I ran down the hallway, and after leaving a quick note for Poppy, I went outside.

As soon as I listened for the breeze, as I always did when I was out, I knew something was wrong. The air was intensified. It wasn't as calm as it should have been. Listening carefully, I thought I could hear a faint whisper.

"Blue." There it was again, and this time I could tell instantly that it was a message from Willow. I took a deep breath and concentrated on where the whisper had originated from. Locating her position, I took to the skies in a whirlwind. When I landed, the twister was obvious, and Willow was struggling.

"Willow, just hold on to me, okay?" I could see the twister in the distance. It was already starting to look and feel like it could be the most powerful I had seen in a while.

"Can't you stop it?" Willow shouted over the noise. I held her hand, but I could already feel her being pulled from me.

"I didn't conjure it," I said helplessly.

"Well, then who did?" Willow shouted.

"I have no idea, but until we find out, we just have to hope it runs its course without too much damage," I yelled back. I looked over Willows's head at the impending disaster. It was a rush of swirling colour as the fallen leaves were swept up in its path.

"Why is it in Ignis?"

"I have no idea," I answered. Both of us watched as a particularly thin-trunked tree was pulled out by its roots. I felt, rather than heard Willows gasp as the tree flew over our heads and landed with a thud in the middle of the Ignis training ground.

"It's okay," I said. "No one was the—"

"Blue. Get down." Willow shouted as she fell to the ground, pulling me with her.

I looked up just as the twister reached us.

I stood up.

"Blue what are you doing?" Willow screamed.

I could feel her pulling on my arm, but I resisted. I could feel the energy pouring from me, but nothing was happening. I couldn't stop it. Willow was still holding my hand, which suddenly felt hot against my skin.

"Willow. No." I shouted my warning a fraction too late and purple flames surrounded us both. The twister sucked in the flames too. It left us behind, but took the flames with it, burning trees as it went. I pulled Willow to her feet. She looked horrified. "Come on, we have to stop it."

We both ran as fast as we could towards the ever-growing twister. It was a terrifying sight, but a blessing that it was happening at the current time of day. If there were people out in the forest at the current time, lives would be lost.

As we were about to gain on the twister, Willow was up in the air. She had conjured a Boobrie and was flying high above me. I watched as she flew above the twister and I stared in horror as she jumped. The Boobrie turned into a whoosh of water which fell into the eye of the twister. The fire was there one minute and gone the next. The impact caused the twister to fizzle out too.

Momentarily, I was too shocked to realise what had exactly happened. I searched the sky for Willow and my heart skipped a beat when I couldn't see her. Suddenly, I noticed a black figure on the ground. I ran over to find Willow collapsed on the ground. Her face was pale, and her skin was cold.

But she was breathing.

CHAPTER THIRTY-SIX
WILLOW

When I woke up, it took me a moment to realise what had happened. The last thing that I could remember was falling.

I looked around me. This wasn't Ignis. I winced as I stood up, my muscles sore from the fall. There were trees all around me, but through the thinner branches, I could see a vast open space just beyond. I walked towards it.

Poira invaded openness. They were transparent, almost invisible versions of their former selves, stuck between this world and the next.

I was in Limbus.

I gasped as I realised that I may not have survived the fall.

I inched closer to the Poira, careful not to touch any of them. Curiously, the Poira didn't seem to notice me, yet they were interacting with each other. Perhaps that meant that I wasn't one of them. Yet.

Something caught my eye on the far side of the clearance. A person. It was a boy and he wasn't Poira. However, as I began to walk towards him, he disappeared. I stopped and stared at the place he was stood just a few seconds ago. I looked around and it was as if nothing had happened. The Poira hadn't even turned in that direction.

I looked to my left at a young girl. She was on the floor playing with a bunch of twigs. She looked to be about six or seven. A Younger who shouldn't be in Limbus, I thought.

I knelt in front of her and waved my hand in her face. Nothing. I got up and continued to walk among the Poira. As I weaved in and out of the transparent figures, I found myself becoming more and more distressed. I didn't know how I had got here, and I didn't know how to leave.

Suddenly, I shivered as my hand brushed the shoulder of an older man sat just to my right. The sensation was strange like I had dipped my hand in a bucket of ice. I pulled my arm away and continued. The vastness in front of me seemed to be growing, the trees behind me looking more like twigs in the distance. I could see no end in sight.

Just when I thought that the day couldn't get any worse, I froze. One of the Poira solidified right in front of me. I had never heard that any of them could do that, not in any of the stories I was told when growing up. I didn't know what it was capable of.

When the Poira turned solid, it seemed to notice me. My eyes widened as I realised that I was in a bad position. The only place to run was back towards the trees, but now there was no cover and the Poira was looking angry, and I was the target.

I began to run back towards the shelter of the thick. The man behind me was middle-aged with a wild-looking beard. His eyes were bloodshot red and his hands were balled up into white-knuckled fists. My heart began to thump loudly, and I was suddenly scared that this would anger the Poira, causing him to become even more violent than he already seemed.

I tripped over my feet, silently cursing myself for my clumsiness. The Poira was gaining on me. He grabbed my leg as I tried to pull myself to my feet and I fell helplessly back to the ground. I covered my face as he fell on top of me, his hands pinning me down.

I waited for it to end, but the Poira was suddenly pulled off me. I moved my arm and looked up. There was a golden glowing before me, separating me from the Poira. The shield was a person and as I squinted through the glow, I managed to discover who was saving me.

"Mom?" I said incredulously.

The woman looked back and smiled. "Run sweetheart. Back to the trees." I stared in disbelief. My world seemed to be crashing down.

"Mom?"

"Willow, run. I can't hold him back for much longer. Run. Now." I did as she asked, occasionally looking over my shoulder. She was still there, holding him back. As I reached the trees, my mom looked towards me. The shield seemed to glow brighter for a second before fizzling out completely. She was gone.

I ran. I continued to run as the tears silently ran down my face. I couldn't comprehend what I had seen. My mom. She was here. In Limbus. Was she dead?

I fell to the floor in a heap and wept. If my mom was here, then what about my dad? Aspen? Forrest? Everybody that had gone missing. What if they were all dead too? I couldn't think. My head was spinning.

CHAPTER THIRTY-SEVEN
BLUE

Carefully, I slid my arms under Willows back and lifted her off the ground. Her head rested against my chest as I began walking back to her house. It was quiet. Everybody was still sleeping.

The ground was a mess. The twister had caused destruction. Trees were uprooted and there were scorch marks all over the ground from the fire. I carried on walking, dodging tree trunks and debris spread all around. I could see Willow's small house in the distance. The sun had fully risen now, a golden glow beaming down on the community. It wouldn't be long until her neighbours would wake from their slumber and come investigating. I had to get Willow inside before that happened.

I reached the door uneventfully and carried Willow to her bedroom. The room still smelt of smoke and the haziness showed that it still lingered. I laid her down on her bed, pulling the covers over her cold body. She was shivering, and I had to convince myself that that was most likely a good thing. She was living, if not fully in the conscious mind.

I did a quick inspection to make sure that there were no broken bones before collapsing into a chair next to the bed. I closed my eyes, finally feeling the effects of the energy that I had poured from my body trying to stop the twister. I shouldn't have bothered, it had only made me weaker.

***

The room was darker when I opened my eyes. I looked out of the window and saw that the community of Ignis had discovered the remnants of the twister. The whole community was involved in cleaning the immediate area. I watched for a while, intrigued that the community had brought it upon themselves to clean up. There were no Tree Leaders in Ignis currently, other than Willow, and she most definitely had not given any orders. I watched in admiration. This is how I hoped Ventus would be one day.

Suddenly, Willow groaned. I walked back over to the bed and sat down. I felt Willows's forehead. It was still very cold to touch, but she had stopped shivering. Her face was twitching as if in pain and her eyeballs were moving beneath her lids. She was dreaming, I realised. I watched her for a while, unsure of what to do. Willow was a mystery to me, one that I couldn't seem to solve. I wouldn't stop trying though.

She opened her eyes and for a moment I stood transfixed, waiting for her reaction. She wasn't moving though, even her eyes were fixed straight ahead staring at the ceiling.

"Willow?" Her eyes scanned the room and finally fixed on me. Her face was expressionless and I suddenly worried that something had happened during the fall. Something that couldn't be fixed. "Willow?" I tried again.

Suddenly, she started thrashing her arms around wildly. She was trying to lift herself out of the bed, the covers were tangled around her body and she was screaming. I moved forward instantly, trying to hold her down.

"Let me go." She shouted at me.

"Willow. No. You are too weak right now." I pinned her arms down to her sides. Already I could feel her getting weaker and her breaths were laboured and ragged. Eventually, she fell back against the pillows and I thought it was safe to let her go.

"Blue? How did I get here?" she asked.

"I brought you here, Willow," I said. She looked confused. More confused than she should have.

"How did you pull me from that place?" she asked quietly. Her eyes were wide, and she looked scared. She also looked upset.

"I didn't pull you from anywhere. When you fell, you were knocked unconscious. I brought you back here. We have both been here ever since." I explained.

"What? I was in Limbus, Blue."

"No, you weren't Willow," I said. I felt a chill overcome me. Had she been that close to death? Had her soul been taken to Limbus?

"It seemed so real," she said. "I saw my mom, Blue." Tears began to fall as she disclosed this information. "Do you think she is dead?" she asked quietly. I sat on the edge of the bed. She was looking at me so innocently. She looked like a little girl.

"Willow, it wasn't real. You were here, and you didn't go anywhere. It wasn't like when you went to the Endarkened. Your body has been here the entire time." I said, urging her to understand.

"Then where are they, Blue? Why haven't we found them yet? It doesn't make sense. Where could they have possibly gone? We must face reality. It is the only plausible solution. They are not coming back." I stared at her. Why was she suddenly feeling so negative? She turned in her bed, her back now facing me.

"I am not going to let you think like that," I said, a little more harshly than I intended. "You need to be positive, Willow. If not for yourself, then for the community you have here in Ignis. They will be looking to you for answers and you need to be ready for that." She didn't show any hint that she had listened to any of my words and instead continued to lie with her back to me.

I sat back in the chair, angry. Angry at myself for putting Willow in that situation. I should have protected her better. I was angry at Willow. She had been so careless, not thinking about herself at all. I was angry at the whole situation and the fact that I could do nothing about it.

I leaned forward, resting my chin on my hand when I noticed something on the floor that wasn't there before. I bent to pick it up. It was a photo.

"Willow, what is this?" I asked. The photo showed a baby. A normal, happy-looking baby. There was a halo of golden light surrounding her though. "Willow?"

"What Blue? What do you want?" She turned to face me, and her face fell when she saw what I had in my hand. "Where did you get that?"

"It was on the floor," I answered. "Who is this?" I felt like I already knew the answer though.

"Do you have to ask? Nothing is normal about me Blue. All my life, I always thought that I never really fit in. Now I know that for sure." She looked up at me, she looked horrified.

"Maybe that is true, Willow."

"You didn't have to agree with me, Blue." She turned away from me again, but I put my hand on her shoulder.

"You didn't let me finish," I said softly. "I said that maybe you don't fit in, but I am certain that you fit in with me." She still didn't turn around. I squeezed her shoulder and she slowly turned towards me.

"How can you be so sure?" she asked.

Her eyes had started to brim with tears as she waited for me to answer. Instead, I pulled her into me. She leant against my chest, she was beginning to warm up now and started to cry.

"I've never been surer about anything in my life," I said. My words were muffled against her hair. I felt her cry harder. "That wasn't supposed to make you cry," I added. She gave out a raspy chuckle as she leaned into me further.

"What are we going to do?" she asked after a while.

"I don't know, Willow. We will think of something." I answered.

I shifted on the bed so that I was leaning up against the wall. Willow followed me. I put my arm around her and she settled down against me. I pulled the covers over us both. A short while later, I felt the steady rhythm of her breathing as she slipped back into sleep.

I held the photo in my hands as Willow slept, silently studying it. I had never seen anything like it and I made a note to talk to Poppy about it. She was obsessed with witch magic and I was sure that this would be very interesting to her. If Willow had necromancy in her blood, which I strongly suspected that she did, this photo could explain a lot.

I leaned my head back against the wall. It felt right, holding Willow in my arms. If only I could get the other Tree Leaders to understand.

CHAPTER THIRTY-EIGHT
WILLOW

"Blue, there is something that I haven't told you," I said quietly.

"Hmm?" he mumbled sleepily. He squeezed his arms tighter around me.

"I think I saw my uncle," I said.

"I didn't know you had an uncle?"

I took a deep breath. "He was in the Endarkened." I could feel his body tense behind me. "Blue?"

"Willow, why didn't you tell me?" I expected him to sound angry, but his voice was soft. Gentle. I shrugged, unable to find the words. I had prepared myself for an argument, not this. "You know that you can tell me anything," Blue said as he took my hands, his thumbs gently caressing my fingers. "Is this why you've been a bit quiet?"

I nodded. We sat quietly on the bed for a while. The silence was deafening, and Blue wasn't giving away how he truly felt about the fact that I had not told him before now.

"How do you know he was your uncle?" Blue asked.

"I could tell. I honestly thought I was looking at Aspen. When I got back home, I remembered that my dad had a brother." I explained.

"What happened to him?"

"Nobody ever found out," I said. We were both quiet for a while.

"Maybe there is a picture of him somewhere," Blue suggested.

"That is what I thought too," I said. "I couldn't find any though."

"Do you want me to ask around? Maybe one of the other Tree Leaders knows about him."

"No, I think that would open up too many questions."

"Okay." Blue squeezed my hand. "Willow, it is getting late."

I turned my head towards him. He was warm, and the steady beating of his heart was comforting. I didn't want him to leave.

"I know," I said.

"Poppy will be worried. I have to go home."

"Okay."

"You have to get off me," he said, chuckling to himself. "I will come back in the morning, I promise."

"You are so comfy though," I whined.

Blue leant down from his sitting position and kissed me on the forehead. He got up off the bed and collected his jacket off the chair as he did so.

"I'll be back in the morning. No heroics until then, okay?" he said.

"No promises," I replied. Blue sighed as he left the room. "Goodnight," I called.

"Night," he shouted back.

I smiled into my pillow. It had been a long time since I had felt contented. I was happy. Slowly, I got up off the bed. My muscles were sore, and I winced as I stretched my legs out. I walked over to my window and looked outside, assessing the damage. It wasn't too bad. Blue had said that the community had pulled together to clean up the debris. I had no idea how bad it had been though.

The sun was starting to set, and already I was feeling tired even though I had slept all day. Whenever I closed my eyes though, I struggled to get the image of my mom out of my head. The way that the Poira had run after me was terrifying, but I seemed to have a guardian angel at my side. My mom. I just didn't know if I could think of her that way. I didn't want to admit that she was in Limbus. I didn't want to admit that I hadn't got to her in time, that I hadn't saved her.

I went back down and sat on my bed. My stomach was gurgling the most intense of gurgles, but I couldn't find the energy to fix myself anything to eat. Instead, I lay down and closed my eyes. I was almost asleep when I heard a noise outside.

I went back to the window and peered out. It was almost dark already, the sun setting quicker than usual. I couldn't see anything, so I walked out of my room and to the back door. I opened it to look outside. Canvassing the area, I was unable to see anything, but as I was about to go back inside, something caught my eye.

I squinted, trying to see through the darkness. It looked like my mother.

"Mom?" I said. The woman continued to watch me. she was just inside the thick of trees. She didn't move. I moved closer. "Mom?" She turned away from me and began to walk in the opposite direction. I followed her.

She was walking slowly. I walked at an equal distance behind her. I didn't want to chance to catch up to her and to spook her. I took in her long wavy brown hair that fell halfway down her back and the way she walked with a slight limp. My mother had teleported badly one day landing awkwardly on her leg. It had never healed properly.

We walked for what seemed like miles when the woman stopped. When my mom stopped. I looked around and took in the now-familiar resting place. It kept popping up whenever anything happened. Today though, the resting place was occupied.

The young woman standing in the clearing looked delighted to see me. Her face was porcelain white like a dolls face, and her brown hair shimmered with the moonlight. It fell around her shoulders in waves.

She clicked her fingers and my stomach lurched as my mother disappeared before my eyes. "Mom?" I shouted. "Mom?" I searched, but she was gone. "Where is she? What have you done to her?" I shouted at the woman.

"That wasn't your mother, child," she said. Her voice was soft and gentle. I felt my anger subside slightly. "That was a Tunda." She said matter-of-factly.

"A Tunda?" I asked, confused. I had heard of them but never seen one before. Well, I thought I hadn't.

"Yes, dear. I use Tunda to get what I want. I needed you here, therefore I thought a double of your mother would get you here. I was right." She explained.

"Why do you need me?" I asked. I had no idea who this woman was.

"All in due course. Firstly, I wanted to meet you. I have waited a long time for this day to come."

"Why? Who are you?" I asked.

"I am Hazel." She replied.

I looked at her in disbelief. Hazel. The witch? I had no idea. She didn't look like a witch.

"Ridiculous," I said. "That is impossible."

"Is it? I didn't put up much of a fight when they banished me to this hellhole. I knew I would get out. It was only a matter of time. I had, let's say, an insurance policy ensuring that I would make it out."

"What kind of insurance policy?"

"You will find out soon enough."

CHAPTER THIRTY-NINE
BLUE

As soon as the sun had risen, I was out of the house. I decided to walk over to Ignis. I couldn't stop thinking about Willow through the night which resulted in me getting very little sleep. The weather was clear today, and crisp. The fog seemed to have subsided and hadn't reached the border of Ignis or Terra. Perhaps Poppy had been right, and the unbalancing had righted itself.

The trees had grown thinner now, the effects of the twister imminent. I made a mental note to visit Terra and ask them to help with the replanting. Ignis seemed different with so few trees.

I continued my way, enjoying the fresh air as I reached the community. I was walking towards Willows house when I spotted a young girl standing at the edge of the forest.

"Acacia?" I said. She turned around. She looked stricken. "What's wrong?"

"It's Willow," she said, looking towards the forest. I followed her gaze, a sinking feeling in the pit of my stomach.

"She has gone in there, hasn't she?" Acacia nodded. "When?" I asked.

"After dark, last night," Acacia replied.

"After dark? Why didn't you stop her?" I said angrily. Acacia recoiled, clearly afraid. "I'm sorry," I said more softly.

"I didn't go after her because of the curfew," she said.

"What curfew?"

"The one that Willow instigated," Acacia said.

I thought back to mine and Willow's previous conversations. I couldn't recall her ever saying anything about a curfew.

"Why?"

"When Fern got hurt, Willow said that it wasn't safe for us to be out after dark unsupervised," she explained.

"Fern got hurt?" I said, trying to clarify what had happened.

"Yes, she was attacked by a Superno."

"Shadow or Aurora?"

"Shadow."

"You're certain?" I asked. Acacia nodded. "Why wouldn't Willow tell me?" I wondered out loud.

"I don't know," Acacia answered. "Now Willow is out there all alone and has been all night. You have to do something, Blue." Acacia looked panicked again.

"Okay, I'm going to go and look for her. Don't worry, I am sure she is fine." I squeezed Acacia's shoulder before I headed towards the thick of trees.

As I reached the thickest branches, I looked back. Acacia was still there, watching. She looked close to tears but there was nothing I could do. I couldn't be in two places at once and I had a feeling that Willow needed help.

The forest was unusually quiet. Now and again, I saw a pair of red eyes staring through the shadows. Superno. What I wanted to know though, was where were all the Aurora Superno? Their job was to keep the Shadow Superno in check. To stop accidents happening. What happened to Fern shouldn't have happened and I was determined to find out why.

A crunch behind me made me spin around. I couldn't see anything, so I continued walking towards the place where I knew Willow was bound to be.

I could hear voices up ahead. They were muffled and barely audible. I walked forward, straining my ears to hear what the voices were saying when I suddenly heard the word Tunda. I froze. If I had heard it correctly, I knew exactly why Willow had gone into the forest after dark.

The Tunda could transform into anyone. Even a loved one. My parents used to tell us stories, like fairy-tales, where the Tunda were known as doppelgangers, a replica of a person. If Willow had seen her mother or father, or even Aspen, she would have followed them without a doubt.

Creeping forward, careful not to step on any branches, I inched closer. That is when I saw her.

CHAPTER FORTY
WILLOW

Hazel looked behind one of the large rocks that were situated next to the border. I looked behind her and noticed something stirring in the leaves on the ground. But before I could determine what it was, Hazel bent over and picked it up. I was horrified to see that it was a young boy.

"What are you doing?" I said, scared for the boy. I had no idea what Hazel was capable of, but I knew it couldn't be good. She didn't answer me, instead, she threw the boy to the ground in front of us. He was young, about ten. I didn't recognise him. He wasn't from Ignis.

"I need his soul, child," Hazel said as if it was the most normal thing in the world.

"You can't," I said in fear. Hazel ignored me though as she knelt on the floor beside the boy. He was writhing as if in agony, but he wasn't making a sound.

I watched in horror as Hazel began sucking the soul from her latest victim. I could see the young boy's soul being pulled from his body, a transparent form lifting into the air. It was as if Hazel was a magnet and the soul was drawn to her. She didn't seem to be making much of an effort either. It seemed like second nature to her as she bent over the body. I had no idea how she was doing it, perhaps it had something to do with the way I had drained Blue's energy that day of the earthquake.

I scrambled backwards on the ground using my hands frantically to move faster as I watched the boys soulless body fall to the floor.

"Please, don't hurt me," I begged.

Hazel laughed. "He will be alright when he wakes up."

"He no longer has a soul," I said. "He won't be okay at all," I added remarkably. How could she think that?

"Of course, he will, you don't need a soul to survive, child."

"It makes you who you are though," I said.

"Yes, well, I need it more than him at any rate." Hazel snapped.

"Why?" I asked.

"To survive." She replied. I didn't know what to say.

I stared at her in amazement. "Did you take my parents' souls?" I asked, unsure whether I wanted to know the answer. Hazel stared at me. "You did, didn't you?" I said, quite loudly.

"It was necessary." I felt my body go weak. When I saw my mother in Limbus, it was real. She was there, her soul anyway.

"Aspen?" I said quietly.

"I have Aspen," she said. "He is still with us. I haven't harvested his soul. Yet." She looked gleeful. It was as if my pain made her happy and she would do anything to keep it that way.

"Give him back," I demanded. I stood up from the cowering position I had yielded to, determined to face the woman who had kidnapped my family.

"You can have him back," she said simply. I stepped back in surprise. "After you have done me one little favour." She added.

"Why would I do you a favour?" I asked.

"Because child, I have something you want. You? You have something I need."

"What is that?"

"Power."

"I don't know what you are talking about," I said, defensively.

Suddenly, I heard a noise behind me, and then I felt it. That familiar presence that had become such an important part of my life. I abruptly had a terrible sinking feeling in my stomach. If only I had learned to communicate the way that Blue could. I could warn him.

"I don't think so," Hazel said in disgust, and before I could stop her, a bright white light erupted around her. It powered towards me and I covered my head with my hands.

CHAPTER FORTY-ONE
BLUE

I dropped to the ground as the blinding white light flew towards me. I tried to teleport, but my abilities were not working so I covered my head as I braced myself for the impact that would inevitably come. As the light reached me I felt a burning sensation over my skin, but as quick as it had come, the burning stopped and the light disappeared.

Slowly, I lifted myself to my feet to discover complete darkness. I couldn't see anything in front of my face, let alone Willow or the woman that she was speaking to.

"Willow?" I shouted. There was no answer. I moved forward, snapping branches under my feet as I walked. It was then that I noticed them. The eyes.

Bright red eyes stared at me from all directions and suddenly I was frozen to the spot where I stood.

Superno.

There was a miraculous number of Shadow Superno surrounding me, more than I had ever seen. The Aurora Superno should have stopped this many from multiplying. Maybe it had had something to do with the unbalancing.

I was scared to move, but I had to find Willow. I could no longer sense her location. It was obvious that she had teleported away from the area, but I needed to be closer to her to find her.

A growl emanated from behind me and I sunk to the ground. An intense pain shot through my arm as I shook a Superno off. I looked down to see the razor-sharp teeth marks that covered my arm which slowly covered with blood. The metallic smell seemed to attract the rest of the Superno that surrounded me. My blood ran cold as I tried desperately to teleport.

Another Superno grabbed at my ankle. Fortunately, it didn't manage to get a good hold and only grazed the skin. I couldn't feel any blood seeping as I had in my arm, which was now dripping continuously onto the ground surrounding me.

I tried my abilities again. A breeze erupted from me and for the first time in a while, I felt hope. I tried to forget the Superno who were undoubtedly getting ready to pounce and focused on teleporting away from the area.

CHAPTER FORTY-TWO
WILLOW

I could hear Blue calling out for me in the darkness. I was still stood in the same position as I had been a moment ago, but I was unable to move. My legs were frozen, not literally, but in fear of what would happen if I moved.

I needed to get rid of the darkness, and then I felt it, the power beginning to surge through me. I felt it move from somewhere within me and my fingers began to tingle. I gasped as the white light that had surrounded us before began to reappear. A short distance in front of me, Hazel began to laugh.

"You dare to use my powers against me?" She laughed harder as the darkness disappeared altogether.

I looked at her across the clearing. She looked smug as she raised her eyebrows. I turned to look in the direction that Blue had come from, but he was gone.

"Where is he?" I demanded.

"How should I know? He probably got knocked off his feet from the blast," she shrugged.

"I need to go and find him."

"I don't think so," Hazel said, and suddenly she was next to me, holding on to my arm. There was a whirl of darkness and when our feet touched the ground, we weren't in the clearing anymore. We were in a cave. It looked eerily familiar.

"Where are we?" I asked.

"My resting place, of course," Hazel said irritably as if I should have known.

I looked around. It was just how I had dreamed it with the only difference being that the cave was alight. Some torches lined the rocky walls and led the way through the corridor to what I remembered to be the clearing at the end.

"Limbus," I said.

Hazel nodded. "Partly. I created Limbus before my entrapment many years ago. It was somewhere I could keep an eye on the souls that I pertained."

"Why?" I asked.

"I needed souls to stay youthful. If I didn't, I wouldn't die, but I would become a withered old woman, and who wants that?" she said.

"You are hurting people though. Do you not care?"

"The soulless bodies are kept very safe at the other end of this corridor. It is like they are sleeping if you must be reassured. The Poira are in no pain." she explained.

"I'm not just talking about the Poira. I'm talking about their families. People are searching for their missing loved ones. They are hurting. I have done nothing but search for Aspen and my parents." I said as I got more wound up. Hazel didn't look the least bit concerned. She looked almost bored.

"That is none of my concern. I have a need and I am fulfilling that need."

"You don't care at all," I said incredulously. "I want to leave. Get my brother, as you promised."

"I said that I would give your brother back in exchange for a favour. You haven't done that yet." she sneered.

"Fine. Then I will just find him myself."

I pushed past Hazel towards the end of the caved corridor. I came face to face with the clearing in which I was almost attacked by the Poira. Aspen wouldn't be there. Hazel had said that much herself.

I turned around and ran in the opposite direction. Running past Hazel was sickening. Her face said it all. She was enthralled as she watched me look for Aspen like I was playing a game of hide-and-seek. I reached the mouth of the cave and came to a halt.

There were bodies upon bodies upon bodies that lined the walls and the floor, and they were piled on top of each other. Hazel was right. They did look like they were sleeping, but the sheer magnitude of bodies showed just how many people Hazel had kidnapped in the past. None of the missing persons from before had been found and there were hundreds of them.

"Are all these people in Limbus?" I wondered out loud.

"They are." I jumped as Hazel appeared next to me. She looked out into the cave, which was vast in size, almost proudly. She was admiring her work.

"This isn't right. You must know that." I tried again.

"Look, I haven't hurt anybody. They are fine."

"They don't have souls," I said. "How are they fine?"

Hazel just shrugged, turned around and walked back in the other direction. I stared after her. I scanned the bodies nearest to me. I couldn't see Aspen or my parents. I looked for Forrest too, but I couldn't see him either. Maybe that was a good thing.

CHAPTER FORTY-THREE
BLUE

After teleporting to the outskirts of the clearing, I still had a clear view of Willow and the woman. I saw Willow look back towards where I had been standing before.

After a few seconds, I watched amazed as the woman strode to Willow in a matter of seconds in a whirlwind of darkness. She grabbed Willows arm and then they were both gone.

"Willow?" I shouted.

Silence.

CHAPTER FORTY-FOUR
WILLOW

"If you have my parents, then where are they?" I demanded as I followed Hazel down the passageway.

"In a safe place," Hazel replied.

"Prove it," I said. "I need to know that they are okay."

She stopped about three-quarters of the way towards Limbus and clicked her fingers. I looked around, frantically trying to see what she had done.

Suddenly, out of the corner of my eye, I saw a transparent form start to appear out of thin air. My eyes widened as I saw first my mother appear before me, and then my father materialised after. My mother was just as I had remembered her in Limbus. They were both smiling at me.

"Mom? Dad?" Their eerie forms continued to look at me. "Why aren't they doing anything?" I asked Hazel.

"They can't do anything. They can't speak. They can only barely move. They are soulless, child. What part of soulless do you not understand?" Hazel snapped.

"Can't you bring them back? Put their souls back in their bodies?" I asked.

"No, I cannot. If I do that, my youthfulness will start to fade. I have worked too hard to reverse the work I have done."

I reached out to touch my mom's arm. My fingers slipped straight through her.

"You cannot touch her," Hazel said lazily.

"Where are their bodies?" I asked.

"Through here," she said.

I looked to where she was indicating and noticed a very small gap in the cave wall. I followed her direction and squeezed through. Beyond the wall, space expanded tremendously. Lying in the centre of the floor were my parents. They looked as if they were sleeping. They looked content.

"Why are they asleep?" I asked Hazel through the gap in the wall. "You said that the soulless could live as normal without a soul. Why are all these people asleep?"

Hazels face appeared in the gap. "They can live somewhat ordinary lives. They would have no empathy or could barely perform ordinary tasks. I couldn't very well have an army of soulless bodies traipsing through the Zones, could I? Believe it or not, I am not a monster. I wouldn't put my community through something like that."

I could barely come up with a reply to that. She was delusional.

"Now," Hazel said. "Back to our little task at hand." She clicked her fingers and suddenly the small cave was occupied with another person.

"Willow? What is happening?"

"Forrest?" I looked from Forrest to Hazel. She looked gleeful.

"What am I supposed to do?" I asked.

"Simply kill the boy."

"What? No? I can't do that. Why would I have to do that?" I shouted weakly. Hazel stared at me, a smirk appearing at the sides of her mouth. "Tell me," I shouted.

"I need to see just how powerful you are, my dear child. I need to see the energy that pours from you as you take this boy's life."

"I am not doing that," I said adamantly.

"Very well," Hazel said as she clicked her fingers.

A fire erupted in the small room we were enclosed in. I looked on in horror as my mothers' body went up in flames. I flung myself on top of her, desperately trying to douse them. It was no use, the fire flared higher than ever. I stepped back, the flames beginning to burn my skin. A few moments later, the place where my mother's body had lain was now a pile of bones. The flames extinguished.

I fell to my knees, clutching my chest, and screamed.

CHAPTER FORTY-FIVE
BLUE

I fell to my knees clutching my chest tightly, trying to ease the tight, searing pain that had come on so suddenly. Blood seeped from my arm, covering my clothes in the sticky, red substance.

A tugging sensation gripped at me, it was pulling me towards an unknown location. I scrambled to my feet and followed the pull.

Willow.

Halfway across the clearing, I could feel her. She wasn't far, and I knew that I could teleport straight to her.

CHAPTER FORTY-SIX
WILLOW

Bringing the knife down, I cringed as I felt it pierce the flesh.

Forrest screamed.

The tears ran down my face as I brought the knife down repeatedly. Warm blood splattered over my body, my face and my clothes. My hands were soaked red. Hazel was laughing behind me.

I hung my head in shame. I couldn't believe that I had just done that. I never thought that I could do something like that.

"What the hell, Willow!"

I looked up into Aspen's face. Hazel had disappeared. He looked furious and his eyes were wide with fear. I followed his gaze down to the pool of blood that had now spread around me. I was about to explain when Blue burst through the cave door behind Aspen. I saw him hesitate for a second before walking closer.

"Aspen, she didn't have a choice," he said carefully.

"What do you mean? Of course, she had a choice." Aspen said angrily, turning on Blue. "You weren't even here. How could you possibly know?"

"I know Willow. She wouldn't do this if she had any other choice." Blue said.

"Well, I thought I knew my sister. I don't know who that is." Aspen said sharply.

I looked up at them both. "Mom is dead," I said, quietly.

"What?"

"She is dead, Aspen. Gone."

I watched Aspen look around. His gaze fell on our father, still lying beside me. Then on Forrest who was lying dead in front of me. I suddenly realised that I was still holding the knife that Hazel had placed in my hand. I dropped it with a clatter causing blood to spatter everywhere. Aspen left the small enclosure, leaving Blue and me alone.

"Willow, are you okay?" Blue said.

"No, I'm not okay, Blue. You need to leave. You can't be around me. I am not good for you. I will only drag you down with me."

"If I could, I would walk away, Willow. I would do anything for you. What I won't do though is leave you here, in this state, despite how much you protest."

Blue looked at me with such fierceness in his eyes that I thought he might try and push me away. Instead, he just closed his eyes as if in defeat. He was knelt next to me now, his knees squelching in blood.

"Blue—"

"You need to awaken a stronger power. You must reach deep down. Deeper than you have reached before. It is there. You just have to find it." Blue said. "Do not let this beat you, Willow. You have got too much to live for."

"What have I got to live for Blue? My mother is dead, my father has no soul and my brother hates me." I said angrily.

"You have me," Blue said. "I am not going anywhere. We fit Willow. You have to believe that, and I won't stop trying to convince you."

I couldn't say anything to him. What could I say? He was still willing to stand by me even though I had just killed an innocent boy.

"Willow, come on. We need to get out of here."

I looked down at my father and Forrest. "I can't just leave them here."

"We will come back for them and we will find a way to bring your father back, I promise. It's not safe here and we need to leave."

Reluctantly, I rose to my feet taking Blues outstretched hand. "What am I going to say to Acacia?"

"We will figure it out."

CHAPTER FORTY-SEVEN
BLUE

When we got back to Willows house, the atmosphere was tense. Aspen had followed us back, but he hadn't said a word. I could tell that Willow wanted to talk to him, but he was having none of it. he wouldn't even look in her direction.

"Blue?" Willow said, breaking the silence.

"Yes?" We were sat in the kitchen at the table, side by side, with Willow leaning up against me. We were both still covered in blood. I had put a bandage over my wounds. My abilities would heal them in time.

"What is going to happen now?"

I thought for a moment before answering her. "We will have to call a meeting at Crownfire," I said. "They need to know what is happening with Hazel."

I couldn't believe it when Willow had described Hazel and all she had done. I didn't think that she could come back.

"What about Forrest?" she asked. Her voice broke as she said it.

"They will need to know," I said. "Willow, I will make it clear that you weren't of sound mind when it happened. Hazel had manipulated you. She killed your mother in front of you."

"That doesn't make what I did right, though."

"Willow, if I was in your position I would have done the same thing."

Willow didn't say anything further. Instead, she got up off the chair and walked over to the mirror in the hall corridor. I watched as she stared at herself in the mirror.

"I'm never going to speak to her again," she said. "Every time I look in the mirror, that is all I will see."

"What do you mean?" I asked.

"Every time I look in this mirror, I will see a killer. I will never forget the way my mother burned in front of me. I will never forget the anger I felt and the despair when I drove that knife through Forrest's heart."

"Willow—"

"I don't know how you can bear to be in the same room as me."

"Willow," I said softly. I walked over to her. I stood behind her and wrapped my arms around her waist. I looked in the mirror. We looked a mess, the both of us, and Willow looked tired and withdrawn.

"Blue, I don't deserve your kindness. I have done a terrible thing and I should suffer for it."

I dropped my arms to my sides. "Willow, will you please listen to me?" She was quiet. "It wasn't your fault."

"Of course, it was." We both turned to find Aspen at the threshold of his bedroom. I didn't know how long he had been standing there.

"Aspen—"

"No Blue. Stop making excuses for her. Nobody made her kill Forrest. She did that all on her own."

"Aspen," Willow shouted. "That witch killed our mother. She was about to kill dad, I didn't have a choice."

"You did have a choice, Willow. Odds are she is going to kill dad anyway. You didn't have to murder Forrest at all."

"How can you say that?"

"We have to face reality, Willow. Stop living in the clouds. She will murder everybody in that cave and you know it."

I stood watching them both. It was a slanging match between the two of them. I watched as Willows's eyes teared up and she ran past Aspen and me into her bedroom, slamming the door behind her.

"Aspen, stop being so hard on her," I said.

"You need to stop talking, you have overstepped your mark here. You are too involved. You know that this thing between you two can't happen. If the Tree Leaders find out, you will both be punished, even exiled. Is that what you want?"

I looked at him incredulously. "She has been through a lot since you were gone. She needs your support now more than anything."

"In case you had forgotten, I lost my mother too. I have probably lost my father. Who is around to support me? Hmm?"

"Willow is around to support you. I know how you feel. I lost my parents too, but Poppy was there. She helped me through a lot, and vice versa."

"Your sister isn't a murderer," Aspen said quietly. He turned around as he walked into his room and shut the door behind him.

CHAPTER FORTY-EIGHT
WILLOW

I heard Blue leave through the back-kitchen door right after Aspen shut his bedroom door. I went to the window and peered out. I watched him teleport in a whirlwind right outside the door. He was covered in blood and I was sure that he would have some difficult questions to answer when he got home.

I saw Acacia open her front door and look over. I closed my curtains quickly and sat down on my bed. I couldn't face her. I couldn't lie, but I couldn't tell her what had happened either. How was I supposed to do that?

I heard Aspen moving around in his room, but I couldn't bear to face him either. It was obvious that he hated me and nothing that I said or did was going to change that. I looked at my hands covered in blood. I could barely move them the blood was so thick and dry. I went into the bathroom.

The water was warm as it covered me, head first. I watched the blood falling into the bottom of the bath and down the drain. I don't know how long I had stayed in the shower for, but suddenly there was a bang at the door.

"Are you almost done in there, Willow?" Aspen shouted.

I jerked out of the mental state I was in. "Erm, yeah. Five minutes, okay?"

He didn't answer me. I grabbed a cloth off the side of the bath and began wiping down my arms, scrubbing at the crusted blood that was stubborn to the hot water. Satisfied, I turned the shower off and grabbed a towel.

I opened the door slowly, expecting to see Aspen on the other side, but he wasn't there. I went into my room, closing the door behind me. it was then that I heard the bathroom door close as Aspen went inside. He didn't want to see me.

I felt a little more human as I dried and dressed. I opened my curtains and looked outside. The sun was shining. It was another day like nothing had happened. According to the Youngers outside playing, it was just a normal day. I had a feeling that it wouldn't last. Hazel had resurfaced and from what I could tell already, it wasn't a good thing.

***

It was dark the next time I left my room. I walked into the kitchen after I had heard Aspen moving around and then the smell of food. My stomach grumbling had forced me to face him. Aspen was sat at the table with a bowl of soup in front of him.

"There is more in the pot," he said, pointing to the stove.

I smiled gratefully and went to fix myself a bowl. A sat opposite him and quietly ate my soup. I glanced at him every few minutes, but he was fixated on his supper. He looked thinner and older. I could only imagine what horrors he had been through.

"Aspen?"

"Not yet Willow. I need more time," he said sharply. I shut my mouth and continued to eat my supper. Thankfully, Aspen didn't leave the room as he had been doing.

We carried on eating in silence until Aspens chair shifted backwards as he rose to put his dish in the sink.

"Willow?" I turned around, surprised. "There is a Crownfire meeting at first light. Be ready, okay?" I nodded.

Aspen didn't know that I couldn't hear the calls from Crownfire. It was a good job that he had said something.

CHAPTER FORTY-NINE
BLUE

"First light, again? Really?" Oakley bellowed as everybody's platform locked into place.

I looked around at the other Tree Leaders, most looked bored rather than concerned. I looked over at Willow and Aspen. They were standing as far apart as they could from each other. Aspen at least looked as if he didn't want to kill Willow anymore. There was some tension there though.

"Blue, could you please tell us the nature of this meeting?" Dune asked.

"Hazel," I said.

"Why would you bring her up?" Lily asked.

"She has returned," I said simply.

It was only Willow, Aspen, Poppy and myself that didn't seem perplexed by that information. Dune and Lily visibly gasped, Oakley tried not to recoil and Crimson was stood behind him as usual, not saying a word.

"That is preposterous," Oakley said.

"It is true," Willow said. Everybody turned to look at her.

"Aspen?" Dune said surprised as if he had only just noticed him. "You have returned. Where have you been, may I ask? You have missed many meetings."

Aspen looked uncomfortable. "I was kidnapped."

"Kidnapped by whom?" Lily asked.

"Hazel," he said. The other Tree Leaders looked at each other.

"Do you expect us to believe that?" Oakley boomed. "Did you all make this nonsense up to make us believe that a witch from eighteen years ago has returned? It is ridiculous."

The Tree Leaders looked from me to Willow and Aspen.

"He is telling the truth," I said.

"Do you have any proof, Blue?" Dune asked.

"I saw her, at her resting place. She was very much alive." I explained.

"This is not something to be taken lightly," Dune said. "I would like to see this resting place for myself."

I nodded. "Very well, I will take you there myself," I said. "There is something else." I hesitated. "Forrest, the Younger from Ignis, is dead." I felt Poppy tense beside me, I had failed to mention the news about Forrest to her.

"Dead?" Lily exclaimed. I nodded. "How?"

"Hazel," I said. I looked over at Aspen and Willow. Aspen was just looking down at his feet. Willow looked as if she was about to say something.

"Don't say a word," I said through the wind.

"Why aren't the flames sparking red?"

"Because I am not lying, Hazel did kill him. She manipulated you, Willow. That death is on her."

Willow nodded across Crownfire. She didn't say a word and I breathed a sigh of relief when Aspen kept quiet as well.

"Does the family know?" Dune asked.

I shook my head. "No. Although his sister is extremely eager to find her brother. I think they need to be told sooner rather than later."

"Very well, you and I will visit Acacia and her mother on the way to the resting place," Dune said, talking to me. I was glad in a way that the others were not invited. Oakley would be a nightmare. "Dismissed."

***

I waited for Dune after the platform descended. I didn't go over to talk to Willow, although I could see her loitering on the neutral ground near Ignis.

"Don't worry," I sent through the wind. I saw her relax as my message reached her. She looked across at me.

"That is a difficult request."

"I know. Just go home. Dune and I will be there shortly to talk to Acacia and her mother. You need to be there. They will need you." She nodded.

"Blue, are you ready?" I jumped as Dune appeared behind me, not hearing him as he had walked towards me. I nodded.

We teleported straight into the Ignis community. It was a very different experience teleporting through the ground. Dune was from Terra and his abilities involved the earth. The hole appeared in the earth above us as we had ascended the ground. I looked down to see the hole repair itself as Dune brushed the dirt from his clothes. He looked at me.

"A little messy, but convenient," he said smiling. I smiled back.

"It is that house there," I said. I pointed to the small house to the right of Willows. Somebody was peering out of the window. As we walked over, Acacia opened the door.

"Acacia?" Dune asked. She nodded.

I couldn't help but notice curtains twitching and heads peering around corners. The Ignis community had grown used to seeing me around, but Dune was a different matter. Many considered him head of the Tree Council, despite there being a first in each Zone. Dune was different though. "We have some rather bad news, I'm afraid." He said. "Is your mother around?"

"I know that Forrest is dead," Acacia said bluntly.

"Excuse me?" Dune said.

"I know that my brother is dead. I've felt the bond between us shift over the last few weeks. Last night, I felt it break."

"Astonishing," Dune exclaimed.

I nodded. I had never heard of anything like it, although my bond with Willow seemed to be getting stronger and stronger. I could almost always pinpoint her exact location. At least, she sent out some sort of beacon that I could follow.

"I am right, aren't I?" she asked. I nodded, shifting my eyes to the floor.

Acacia sighed. "We better go inside. My mom is in the kitchen."

We followed her slowly, the atmosphere was excruciating. Acacias mother was sat at the table when we entered. She was pale and thin, which I think must have occurred after the disappearance of her son.

"Mom? The Tree Leaders are here." She looked up at us with fear in her eyes.

"I am afraid we have some bad news," Dune said.

I watched and listened as he broke the news to her. I watched as she fell to her knees and I listened as she let out the most painful cry I had ever heard. I couldn't watch it anymore, so I quietly slipped back outside.

About ten minutes later, Dune exited the house. "Are you okay?" he asked.

"I'm sorry," I said. "I found that incredibly difficult."

"I understand." Dune replied. "It is never an easy job to do, but it is a necessary one." He clasped my shoulder. "Let's go and see this resting place, shall we?"

***

Twenty minutes later we were standing in the clearing that had once been Hazels resting place.

"Well…" Dune exclaimed.

"I don't know what happened," I said astonished.

The resting place was a horrific mess. The grass had been ripped from its roots, the leaves were lying dead on the floor and it looked as if the rocks and boulders had exploded. Debris covered the ground and a giant crater had formed in the middle of the clearing.

"It certainly seems clear to me that you are indeed telling the truth. Do you know where Hazel is now?"

I shook my head. "I do not."

"This is a problem," Dune said. I nodded in agreement. "It is imperative that we find her. The destruction that she caused before we trapped her the last time was enormous. We cannot let her roam free again."

"What do we do now?" I asked.

"We need to speak to Aspen. Right now, he is the biggest lead that we have. He was kidnapped by Hazel and he escaped. We can at least ask him how it was that she managed to capture him." I nodded. "Let's go."

"Willow? Can you hear me?" I sent through the wind.

"What's wrong?"

"We are on our way to your house. Dune wants to speak to Aspen. Hazel is gone."

"She's gone? What do you mean?"

"I will explain later."

***

"Aspen, is it alright if we ask you a few questions?" Dune asked.

"Yes, of course," Aspen replied.

We were all sat around the kitchen table. Willow on one side of me, Dune on the other. Aspen was sitting opposite us. It looked almost like an interrogation.

"How did Hazel take you?"

"She sent a Tunda, in the form of my mother," Aspen explained.

Willow grabbed my hand under the table. I squeezed it.

"Naturally, you followed it, I presume?" Dune asked.

"I did."

"I would have done the same, I am sure," Dune said with a reassuring smile. "What happened when you followed the Tunda?"

"It led me to the clearing, the resting place. Hazel was there."

Willow and I listened in silence to the conversation between Aspen and Dune. Willow had laced her fingers with mine and it felt perfect, despite the circumstances.

"What happened next?"

"She teleported straight towards me, grabbing my arm on the way. The darkness followed. That is all I remember until I woke up and saw Willow." Aspen said.

Dune turned towards us. "You were there?" Dune asked her.

"I was. I had a similar experience. I followed a Tunda too. I thought it was my mom. When Hazel teleported me underground, she killed our mom." Willow explained.

"I am very sorry for your loss," Dune said gently. "It is a shame that this is all happening again. We have a distinct advantage this time around though. You have both seen her lair, you know what is there. This could be helpful."

Aspen looked as if he was about to explode, but he seemed to keep his cool.

"Right, I will leave you to it. There will be a meeting to discuss our next steps. I will let you know in due course of the time and day." Dune stood and went to the back door. "Blue, are you coming?"

"Yes, of course," I squeezed Willows hand once more and stood up, already missing the warmth of her hand in mine. "Please let me know if either of you needs anything," I said. They both nodded. I walked over to Dune and we both left the house quickly.

CHAPTER FIFTY
WILLOW

I could smell her before I saw her. Despite her obsession to stay youthful, Hazel didn't care too much about personal hygiene.

I was lying in bed. I had been trying to fall asleep for hours. Taking care of Acacia and her mother had drained me emotionally, but physically I was running on adrenaline. I was concerned that something bad was going to happen with Hazel running around out there.

"Hello, my dear child."

Considering that I was expecting her after the stench I had experienced, I was still shocked to hear her voice.

"Aspen!" I shouted. The witch laughed.

"He can't hear you."

"Is this another dream?" I asked, for although I had dreamt many times of the resting place and Hazels caved lair, including Limbus and the Endarkened, I had never dreamt of Hazel before and it unnerved me to no end.

"I can assure you that this is no dream, child."

"Then why can't my brother hear me?" I asked, suddenly terrified that he was hurt.

"He is fine," she said lazily, obviously seeing the panic in my eyes.

"Then why can't he hear me?" I repeated.

It took Hazel a while to reply and I watched as she slowly moved around to the other side of the bed. She seemed to be taking in every aspect of the room and all the time marking each spot with her eye-watering stench. "He is…indisposed, right now." She looked at me. "Oh, for goodness sake, child, don't look so scared."

"Why shouldn't I be scared? You killed my mother and you turned me into a killer." I shrieked.

"You are being so dramatic," she sighed. "It was all necessary. I had to be sure and now I am."

"You had to be sure of what?" I asked.

"That you were my daughter, of course."

My world seemed to stop spinning at the sound of those words. Had I heard correctly? It couldn't be true. "You're lying."

Hazel laughed. "No, I am not."

"I don't believe you."

"Believe what you like, child. It won't change the facts."

I looked at her with disbelief, but I couldn't help searching her features for some sort of resemblance. Her eyes were purple, like mine, except that they were a lot darker. Other than that, I couldn't see much resemblance at all.

"I have a family," I said. "I already have parents. They have always been my parents."

"Your mother bore you, yes. However, she is not your biological mother. I implanted you within her womb as a gift."

"A gift?"

"You see, after your brother, it was found that your mother could no longer bear children. I made that possible. What they didn't know, however, was that I placed my genes in with your father. You are my daughter."

"Why would you do that?" I asked.

"You were my insurance policy. I knew that the Tree Elders were coming for me, and so I made it possible to return after that happened." Hazel explained.

"How did you know that my mother would get a full pregnancy? You said that my mother couldn't bear children. How did she carry me?"

"I made it so."

"All that work, all that planning, was just a plan to resurrect."

"There wasn't much planning at all. Your parents came to me. I didn't go to them. It worked out perfectly." She looked almost humble.

"Why now? Why have you come back now?"

"When you Awakened, I started to get stronger. Then the hold over me snapped. I was free." She said laughing. "It couldn't have gone better."

"What is wrong with you?" I asked. I was disgusted, and although I hadn't believed her before, I had no doubt now. What reason would she have to lie?

"There is nothing wrong with me. I have nothing against you, child. I am just gaining what is rightfully mine."

"Why through all this destruction? Did you have to kill my mother? Did you have to kill Forrest? Did —"

"You killed that idiot boy." Hazel snarled, interrupting me.

"You made me kill him. You turned me into this. Aspen doesn't even want anything to do with me anymore."

"That is not my problem," she said. "You will notice the similarities between us soon enough, and then you won't want your brother around you anyway. In lives like ours, there is too much destruction, too much power. It's better to cut your losses now."

"What do you mean, 'lives like ours'?" I asked.

She looked at me out of those small beady eyes, which looked strange on a face so feminine and porcelain. "You don't think my daughter shares my abilities? We are more alike than you care to admit."

"The purple flames…" I muttered.

"That's right. Purple. The sign of necromancy. It is in your blood, child, and there is nothing you can do about it."

I couldn't say anything. Everything was beginning to fall into place. The purple eyes, the flames. The abilities of all four Zones and the lightning connection.

"Your eyes will darken in time, and become like mine. The things we could accomplish together will be magnificent."

"I'm not like you," I said.

"Aren't you? You just killed a boy, a Younger no less, that you cared about. You barely even hesitated. It is just the beginning."

I lunged for her before I even knew what I was doing. I was almost upon her, about to grab that long hair that flowed perfectly over her shoulder. She vanished. Her laughter filled the air although she was gone.

I stood watching the place where she was standing just moments ago. The stench still stained the room, but she was most definitely gone. I could not sense her any longer.

"Aspen…" I ran from the room straight down the hallway. When I reached Aspen's door, it was ajar. I burst in expecting to find him gone. Or worse. What I found, however, was Aspen asleep peacefully in bed.

I ran over to him and shook his body.

"Willow, what the hell are you doing?" Aspen shouted. I stilled, barely able to keep the tears from falling.

"You're okay?" I gasped.

"Of course, I am okay. What's wrong with you?" he demanded as he sat up in bed.

"Nothing," I said. "I'm just glad you are okay." I hugged him hard before he could stop me. He didn't say a word but instead allowed me to hug him even though I knew he was uncomfortable.

We used to hug a lot before everything happened and now I wasn't sure that I could rely on him for anything.

"I'm going back to bed," I said. Aspen nodded.

CHAPTER FIFTY-ONE
BLUE

Sitting with Poppy, I could appreciate everything I had. She seemed to ground me, something that I needed occasionally when my wonderings befell me. With everything that had happened with Willow and with what was happening with the unbalancing of the weather and the creatures of the Zones, I needed my sister more than anything.

"Did you see her?" Poppy asked, referring to the witch.

"From a distance."

"What was she like?" Poppy was practically bouncing up and down on her seat, clearly intrigued.

"I don't know. Young." I said. "I didn't get that much of a look at her."

"Young? I thought that she was hundreds of years old?" Poppy asked.

"She is."

"Then how—"

"I don't know Poppy. Could we just sit quietly for a minute? Please." I said, exasperated.

"Sure."

She sat back in her chair and began to hum one of the lullabies our parents used to sing to us.

"Poppy?" I snapped.

"Sorry."

***

About an hour later I found myself wondering outside. The Zone and our neighbouring community were alive with people. Youngers were running around the flowerbeds and the adults were talking to each other in groups. It seemed like a normal day, and none of them knew about Hazel.

"Hi Blue," I turned to see Aviv standing behind me.

"Hello Aviv, how are you today?" I asked. Every time I saw him, he seemed to have grown a little. He was almost as tall as me now.

"I am very well, thank you," he answered. "Are you off to see Willow?"

I did a double-take. "Why would you ask that?"

"Oh, I just noticed that you and she seemed to be a bit chatty."

"When did you notice that?"

Aviv grinned. "At Crownfire."

"Right, well that was just meeting stuff," I said.

"That is exactly what she said," Aviv answered. He turned to leave as if satisfied with my answers. "See you around Blue."

I watched him leave and then began to walk. I knew where I was headed, Crownfire wasn't far and I needed to clear my head.

***

"Blue?" As I reached Crownfire, I was shocked and relieved to find Willow sitting in our spot. I walked over to her and sat down.

"What are you doing here?" I asked. "I thought you would be with Acacia and her mother. Or at least with Aspen."

"Aspen doesn't want anything to do with me. I cannot stay in that house. As for Acacia and her mother, they are better off left on their own for now. Aspen will visit later, I'm sure." She spat those last words out.

"You will both get through this. You are family. He has to see that soon enough." I said trying to soothe her pain.

"Yeah, well I'm not so sure." I placed my hand on hers, but she pulled it away. "Blue, don't."

"Willow, what is wrong, other than the obvious?" I watched her as she turned away. She wouldn't look me in the eye.

"I am not good for you, Blue. I have said it before and I am saying it now. You need to leave. I don't want you here."

"Willow—"

"Leave, Blue!" she shouted.

She couldn't see the hurt in my eyes as I got up off the ground and left her there. I always said that I would leave if she wanted me to. I had no idea how hard it was.

CHAPTER FIFTY-TWO
WILLOW

The next Crownfire meeting was about to begin and I felt the strain before I even got there. Aspen walked quite a way ahead of me through the forest. He hadn't mentioned what had happened the night before.

We were the last to arrive, I noticed, as the platform sent us sky-high and locked into place.

"Good of you to join us," Oakley said, a hint of sarcasm protruding from his mouth.

"We apologise," Aspen said, his head down.

I looked around at the other Tree Leaders until my eyes rested on Blues. What I had done to him was hard. I didn't want to hurt him, but if Hazel was right, I had no choice. It was better to do it now rather than later. His eyes didn't leave mine the entire time that I was staring at him. Life had left them, and that hurt me more than anything else.

"It is not a problem," Dune said. "As you know, we have convened to discuss the next steps to the Hazel situation."

"You are certain, then?" Oakley asked. "That she has returned?"

"It would certainly appear so, yes," Dune answered.

"What do we do about it?" The voice was so quiet that I almost missed it. I looked around to see who had spoken, as did a few of the other Tree Leaders.

Oakley stepped aside, and Crimson moved forward. "What do we do about it?" she repeated. I had never heard her speak before.

Dune cleared his throat. "Erm, well I thought we could try to find out what happened last time. It was around eighteen years ago, there must be somebody around now that knew what the Tree Elders did to stop her."

"I was around," Crimson answered. "My parents died the last time she was at large. Hazel couldn't be blamed as there was no proof, but it cannot be a coincidence."

"Okay," Dune replied. "Crimson, if you could speak to anyone in Glacies that was around and may remember, and of what you remember yourself, maybe we can figure this out." Crimson nodded and stepped back again, silent.

"Surely, we can come up with a better solution than that," Oakley said. I watched Crimson roll her eyes behind him, clearly used to his behaviour.

"Maybe you could have a little more faith in your wife, Oakley." Blue exploded.

"Hold your tongue, boy." Oakley boomed. The flames turned red around us.

"I will not hold my tongue. I am sick of you thinking that you are better than everybody else. You treat your wife like she doesn't even matter, when in fact, if it wasn't for her, you wouldn't be in this council."

"When I get a hold of you…" Oakley snarled. The flames turned black.

"Calm. Down." Dune said. It was quiet, he didn't shout, and he didn't snarl. He was calm. It was all that was needed though. The flames returned to normal.

"Oakley, you are suspended from Crownfire for the next five meetings. Crimson can attend and represent Glacies on her own." Dune said with an air of authority.

"You don't have the power to suspend me," Oakley said sneering.

"I can if the rest of the council agree." Dune replied. He looked around at the rest of us. Blue and Poppy immediately agreed, as did Lily. Aspen also nodded without saying a word. Blue was watching me.

"Do it, Willow. It is what he needs." Blue said through the breeze.

I nodded.

"Then it is settled. I will let you know when you can return, Oakley."

Black flames erupted around us and the look on Oakley's face was thunderous.

"Dismissed."

When our platform had descended, I watched as Oakley formed into a block of ice before us. It melted into water causing Oakley to disappear with it. It was amazing.

"Willow, let's go," Aspen said. He began to walk.

"I'll meet you at home," I said. Aspen shrugged and carried on walking. I needed to take some time. I needed to think.

"Willow?"

I froze as I heard Blues voice behind me.

"Not now, Blue," I said, turning around. "I'm sorry about what happened. It has affected you more than I thought it would. I have never seen you have an outburst as you did up there." I said.

"Willow, I just want to understand. What changed your mind about us. Something must have happened between when I left and when I saw you yesterday. Talk to me," he urged.

"Nothing happened, Blue," I said. I pulled him into the cover of some of the thicker trees. I looked around to check that nobody was around. "I need you, now more than ever, but having you around will kill you."

"How?"

"Me, Blue. I have necromancy magic in my blood. Where do you think I got that from?" I said harshly.

"I have no idea, Willow. It was most probably from a distant relative. It is not unheard of."

"You're wrong," I said.

I went to turn away, but Blue grabbed my arm and pulled me back. "Willow, you can't say something like that and then leave. You need to explain it to me. I am not going to think any less of you if that is what you are worried about."

"Hazel was in my room last night," I said. I couldn't hold it any longer. I had to tell someone. Blue had kept my secrets before.

"What? Why?"

"To tell me that she was my mother," I said simply.

"How?" Blue asked. To his credit, he didn't recoil in horror like I thought he would.

"That is what you ask? How?"

"What else was I supposed to say?"

"I don't know." I shrugged. "Listen, I have to go. I must go home to Aspen and I promised to check in on Acacia. We are having a memorial for Forrest later today."

"That will be nice for them," Blue said. "Willow, please don't shut me out again, I know that everything is freaking you out, but I am here for you. I cannot stress that enough."

"Okay," I said quietly. "Blue?"

"Yeah?"

"Can I have a hug before you go?" He didn't answer me but instead pulled me into his arms.

"Send me a message on the wind, if you need me. I'll be there, I promise." I nodded and turned away.

When I looked back, Blue was still standing there, watching me leave.

CHAPTER FIFTY-THREE
BLUE

I walked back to Ventus. The outburst during the Crownfire meeting was so unlike me and I felt ashamed. I didn't want to be known as that person. That was Oakley's position.

My mind was elsewhere as I walked, I barely noted where I was headed. It was only when I heard a loud crack that I lifted my head. There didn't seem to be anyone around, but when I started to walk again, something snapped, and the noise was prominent.

"Hello?" I said, quietly. Nothing. "Hello?" I said a little louder. I turned slowly in a circle straining to hear even the slightest noise. Then out of the trees shone a little colour. "Poppy?"

My sister moved forward through the trees. At a distance, I could see that she looked different. She wasn't talking, which was a big difference to her usual state. She was also holding herself differently. Usually, Poppy stood straight and had perfect posture. This woman was slouched, and she walked almost lazily.

"Poppy?" I tried again, but she didn't answer. I already knew that it wasn't my sister, but I was intrigued as to why this Tunda was summoning me. I followed her.

We walked back through the neutral territory, past Crownfire and into the trees between Ventus and Ignis. I knew where we were headed, and I knew exactly who would be there.

I was right, and as we walked up to what was once Hazels resting place, I held back. I crouched low trying not to be seen as I watched

Hazel look for me. She was expecting me as she stood on her tiptoes to look behind the Tunda. I crouched lower.

Then I heard her laugh. It was the eeriest, normal laugh, and yet it made me go cold all over and shudder.

"I've been waiting for you, dear." I jumped as the voice behind me whispered in my ear.

I turned slowly to face the witch whom I had been watching. I had not noticed her teleport to me. When I looked back at the clearing, the witch was still there. I looked from one to the other, confused.

"What the—" I stammered.

"Astral-projection, my dear. Now, why don't you be a good boy and come with me? I don't want to make this any harder than it already is." She held out her hand.

I looked at the bony, outstretched fingers. "Why is this hard for you?" I asked incredulously, curiously and trying desperately to stall the inevitable.

"Well, what I mean is that I don't want to make this situation any harder on my daughter. She likes you, I can tell. You are bad for her." Hazel said.

"How am I bad for her? I love Willow," I said, saying the words out loud for the first time. "I would never do anything to hurt her."

"You are stopping her from making the right decision."

"What decision is that?" I asked.

"She was born to work with me. We need to work together. It is the way that was intended, and I intend to uphold that plan." Hazel said as she grew more and more distressed.

"You cannot make her do anything. Willow has a mind of her own, believe me, I know, and she will not be swayed by you."

Suddenly, Hazel let out an ear-piercing shriek and as I covered my ears from the sheer magnitude of the sound, she took the opportunity to grab my arm. Before I knew it, we were spinning through a cloud of darkness and I closed my eyes to the dizziness that overcame me.

When we landed, I could barely walk. We were in the underground cave where I had found Willow. The cave was eerily silent and when I tried to focus on my surroundings, I could see that Hazel and I were alone.

"What do you want with me?" I asked groggily. I felt as though I had just woken up from an intense sleeping session and I was struggling to focus on anything.

"All will become clear in time," Hazel said as she laughed to herself. "I need you out of the way if I am to get Willow to do what I want."

"What do you mean?" I asked as I slumped to the ground. I didn't seem to be in control of my body and I felt like I was fainting. Hazel didn't seem too concerned so it was her doing.

"Now, now, dear boy. There is no need to be scared. There are many like you where you are going. All will become clear very soon."

"Stop this," I shouted, but I was sure I barely whispered the words, as I felt the energy draining from my body and my eyes succumbing to the heaviness of the lids. The last thing I heard was Hazels laughing that seemed to echo through my mind.

CHAPTER FIFTY-FOUR
WILLOW

As I walked towards home, I felt a searing pain shooting through my chest. I fell to my knees, leaves crunching beneath me as I fell. I gasped for air as if I was underwater, clutching my chest as I felt the breath leaving my body in bursts.

I tried to call for help, but there was nobody around. I had to get home to Aspen.

I mustered the strength enough to think about teleporting. I had never done it and I wasn't sure exactly what I was supposed to do.

I thought about moving from one place to another.

I thought about home.

Ignis.

Aspen.

I concentrated on getting there, so I closed my eyes and thought long and hard. The next thing that happened was fire and lots of it. I was surrounded, and it calmed me. I kept thinking. Thinking. Thinking.

The fire moved, and I moved with it. I was swirling in a mass of purple flames and it was only for a split second that I thought of the impact the purple flames would bring to my community.

I saw Ignis ahead of me, the communities were getting closer and as I reached the border of the trees, I stopped my concentration. The flames disappeared, and I fell to the ground.

"Aspen?" I shouted from the trees. "Aspen?" Acacia came running towards me.

"Willow? What happened?" she asked.

"I need to find Aspen. Have you seen him?" I asked, agitated.

"I haven't seen him since you both left this morning for the meeting." She answered. She knelt next to me. "Willow, what can I do?"

"Can you help me back to the house?" I asked.

Acacia nodded and put my arm around her shoulders. I lifted myself off the ground with her help and together we walked towards my house.

Acacia and I looked over at the horizon and I swear that the forest became silent. We watched as the ripple between Sationem and the human realm beyond flickered.

"What is that?" Acacia asked.

"I have no idea," I answered quietly. The sight was mesmerising. The ripple began to flicker different shades of reds, golds and oranges. The brightness becoming stronger and stronger. I shielded my eyes, Acacia doing the same. Suddenly, the sky became dark and I removed my hand from my face.

I stopped breathing.

The ripple was gone.

When we got back to the house, my heart sank.

The door was wide open, and the contents of the kitchen were strewn all over the floor. "Did you see what happened?" I asked Acacia.

"No, I didn't. I don't think anybody did. Nobody has said anything. How could this happen without anyone seeing or hearing?" she wondered out loud.

"I don't know," I said. "Thank you, Acacia. I can take it from here. Go home."

"But, Willow—"

"Acacia, go home. You shouldn't be around here. Something is going on now and it isn't safe."

"What's going on?" Acacia asked, concerned.

"I can't get into it now, I just need you to be careful. Be vigilant. Take care of yourself and your mother, Acacia." She nodded. "Now, go home and don't mention this to anybody. The last thing I need is for more Youngers to come around investigating."

"I won't say anything," she said. "Willow, please be careful. Take care of yourself for once. Okay?" I nodded in answer to her question, and I watched as Acacia left the kitchen and walked back home. I relaxed slightly when she walked through her front door unscathed.

I took a deep breath and walked through the kitchen towards the hallway, dodging glass and debris along the way. The mirror in the hall had been thrown from the wall, the reflective glass shattered over the floor. I stepped on it as I moved forward, the crunching sound loud in the empty house.

The door to my room was open, the top knocked off its hinges. Gingerly, I pushed it open as best as I could, the door squeaking as I did so. My room mirrored the kitchen. The only thing that looked as if it had been untouched was the bed.

I walked over to the bed and my eyes widened as I took in what was placed upon it. The picture. It was face up, my baby-self glowing up at me. However, mine wasn't the only picture on the bed. Next to it was another picture of a baby. This one wasn't me, but it had the same golden glow.

The baby was in a dress, which was the only indication that it was a girl. Her eyes were purple, and the face was unsmiling. I looked at my picture, noting the colour of my eyes. They were the same blue that they had been all my life until I Awakened. There was no doubt in my mind that the other baby was Hazel.

Suddenly, I heard a noise in the kitchen. "Aspen?" I shouted as I ran out of my room. The figure standing near the door was not my brother, but a vaguely familiar face. "I know you..." I said slowly. The boy inclined his head.

"We have met once, yes," the boy said.

"I am sorry, I only remember slightly, and I don't remember your name at all," I said, quietly ashamed about the fact that I was a Tree Leader with such poor memory.

"No worries at all. I am Aviv. Pleased to meet you again." He held out his hand.

"You are from Ventus?" I said. "I remember now. What are you doing here in Ignis?" I asked. I looked at his hand. He lowered it to his side.

"I am not sure. I was drawn here," he said. I didn't ask him what he meant, because I knew exactly what he meant. "You don't seem surprised?" he asked, confused.

"I'm not. I have had similar experiences."

"That reminds me, why haven't the detection alarms signalled that I am here?" he asked.

"I turned them off once when I first became Tree Leader. I guess I forgot to switch them back on." I said. "You shouldn't mention that to anybody though," I added quickly.

"I won't," he said. "What happened here?" he asked, looking around.

"I don't know," I said. "Something weird is happening around here now." Aviv nodded, clearly accepting what I had said.

"Fair enough."

"You should go back to Ventus," I said. "I don't know what brought you here, but if anybody in Ignis sees you, they are going to start asking questions. That is not something that I need right now."

"Okay," he said. "I am leaving." He turned around and walked out of the door, without saying another word.

I watched him leave. He presence was a strange one and I couldn't help thinking that the something weird that was happening concerned him somehow. When I had watched him disappear into the thick, I picked up a chair off the floor and sat down. I couldn't stop the tears from falling.

CHAPTER FIFTY-FIVE
BLUE

When I opened my eyes again, I felt light. I felt lifted. The air around seemed to be of nothing. I took a breath, but I couldn't feel any air entering my lungs. I didn't seem to need it.

I looked around. The clearing was full of people. Transparent people and I had a sinking feeling that I knew exactly where I was.

Limbus.

I remembered the way Willow had described it to me. It was not as vivid as when she had shown me the Endarkened, but her description of Limbus had been pretty spot on.

I looked down at my own body and I was shocked to see that the near-invisible legs belonged to my own body. I held out my arms and saw the same thing. Then it hit me.

I was in Limbus. And I was near death.

Willow had said that she had been solid when she had arrived, and I wasn't stupid enough to know that this situation was completely different. I was a part of Limbus, whereas Willow had just been sent here, able to leave whenever she wanted.

I looked at a little girl to my left. She was sitting cross-legged on the ground fiddling with her shoelace. I shuffled over to her, surprised at the heaviness I felt in my legs. Despite the lightness of the air, I struggled to move just a few inches. It was as if I was anchored to the ground.

"Hello," I said, my voice an echo in the clearing.

The girl didn't look up when I spoke, and I put my hand on hers to find that it went straight through. I couldn't touch her, and she didn't know that I was trying. It became apparent that in Limbus, you could not communicate with each other. It was a horrible realisation.

I turned back around from her and searched the clearing. There were hundreds, maybe thousands of souls contained in Limbus, and not one of them could communicate. Only with themselves.

Slowly, I stood up. The energy it took was intensifying and it took all the strength I had to put one foot in front of the other. I dragged my feet as best as I could. The noise I was making echoed all around, and yet no other soul looked up from what they were doing. I could understand why they were all just sitting around. I guessed that the longer they resided here, the less energy they had. And the more insane they became, I thought.

Suddenly, I noticed a block of shadow ahead of me and I squinted through the bright light to see a person. He was old, bald and seemed irrational. He was solidified, just as Willow had described when she had been here. I watched curiously as he looked from one end of the clearing to the other. He stopped and stared when he saw me, clearly able to identify that I was watching.

He ran towards me

"What is happening?" he cried, as he lunged towards me. I didn't have the energy to duck or jump out of the way. I didn't need to though, I discovered, as he ran straight through me.

I turned as quickly as I could, just in time to see him explode before me. It was as if he vanished in a puff of smoke. There was no blood or bones. He was just gone.

I turned back around and recoiled backwards.

"Aspen?"

CHAPTER FIFTY-SIX
WILLOW

"Don't cry, child." I sucked in my breath as Hazel spoke behind me. I turned to see her standing in the doorway.

"What have you done with my brother?" I demanded. I knew she had done something. "You wrecked my house, and you left this?" I said, thrusting the photograph in her direction. She picked it up off the floor, smiling. "Why?"

"You wanted proof, I gave it to you," she said simply. "You and I are alike. We share the same blood whether you want to acknowledge it or not. I will not continue to try and persuade you. You know, deep down."

Hazel walked over towards me, picking up another chair and sitting down. Her stench overwhelmed me. "You know, it wouldn't hurt you to wash occasionally," I said. Hazel smirked at me.

"It is a downside to soul-stealing," she said. "If I wash, I wash the souls out of my skin. I am not prepared to do that."

"So, you would rather live in that stench?" I asked. Hazel pursed her lips.

"I don't expect you to understand. Not until you fully take a soul."

"I will never do that," I said adamantly.

Hazel raised her eyebrows, it was such a familiar gesture, one I knew well. "You have come close, dear daughter. Don't tell me that you didn't find the feeling exhilarating? When that boy of yours protected you from that earthquake, you took advantage of his strength and his vulnerability around you."

"What?" I said, my heart sinking.

"You know what I am talking about. I felt it on him that day in the clearing. A little of his soul, gone. Then I felt it on you. You have him with you. Even now."

I felt my stomach drop. It explained a lot, like the fact that I could suddenly sense where Blue was and vice versa. I did that, without meaning to. What destruction could I manage if I knew what I was doing? It was too scary to even think about. "I didn't mean to," I said.

"You might not have meant to, but it happened. The power is a part of you, there is no denying that, and there is nothing you can do about it." Hazel said, almost gleefully. She was happy that I was like her.

I sat there, thinking about everything that had happened since my parents went missing, and the fact that most of it were disastrous. I had had more bad luck in the last few months than I had in my whole life. The creatures of the Zones were worsening, multiplying. The more violent creatures coming out of their lairs.

"The unbalancing, it's all because of you, isn't it?"

"At the moment when you Awakened, and that cord that held me down snapped, an unbalance happened. Evil suddenly overwhelmed the good. I am the evil, of course," she said matter-of-factly. "The Superno, the Tunda, and the Umbra multiplied. The good was pushed out further. The weather fairies got weaker and so the elements unbalanced too." Hazel explained. "That is why the ripple has diminished."

"How do we stop it?" I asked.

"Why on earth would we want to stop it?" she asked incredulously. "If we stop it, I am trapped once again, and that is not going to happen, my dear."

I sat there once again, contemplating what she was saying. "Where is Aspen?" I said again, hoping that she would at least answer my question.

"He is in a better place, for now."

"What do you mean?" I asked, suddenly fearful for my brother's life.

"That is none of your concern." Hazel snapped, and as she did purple flames arose around her and I watched in fascination the different hues of purple that surrounded her. Even the smoke that rose from the flames had a purple definition to it. I had never seen it around myself before, but it looked magnificent.

Immediately, I stood up from the table and went outside.

"Where are you going, child?" Hazel demanded as she followed me outside. "What are you doing?"

I ignored her as I found what I was looking for. A breeze. I concentrated hard.

"Blue?" I called through the wind. *"Can you hear me?"* I listened intently, waiting for Blues answer, but it never came. *"Blue?"* I tried again, this time in a more menacing tone, hoping that it would carry further.

"What on earth are you doing?" Hazel exclaimed.

"It is none of your concern," I said, using her own words against her.

I watched as my words made her blood boil. I watched as her knuckles turned white as she fisted her hands together. I couldn't help but get some satisfaction from the fact that I had angered her.

"Willow?" I froze as the familiar voice brought me out of my thoughts. Olive.

"Who is this?" Hazel said. It was a voice I hadn't heard her use before. It was sweet, comforting.

"Hi, I'm Olive."

"Olive, go home," I ordered, as I grabbed her wrist and thrust her behind me.

"Willow, Willow, Willow, don't be so rude. Introduce me to your friend." Hazel said. Her voice might have been sweet, but her eyes said a different story and they were menacing.

"This is Olive," I said. "Olive, this is Hazel."

"I haven't seen you around before," Olive said.

"Likewise," Hazel answered.

"Blue? I need you. Now." I tried again, but it was no use. He would have answered by now if he had heard me. He promised. Suddenly, I was angry.

"Come here, dear. Let me see you properly." Olive walked over to Hazel, but before I could stop her, Hazel had grabbed her arm.

In a split second, Olive was on the floor. I looked down in defeat, and I was shocked to see that Hazel hadn't taken Olives soul.

She had taken her life.

CHAPTER FIFTY-SEVEN
BLUE

"Aspen?" I repeated, incredulous.

Aspen was looking around him, clearly surprised as to where he was. He had his arms out in front of him, examining, just as I had. He didn't seem to be taking much notice of me. He looked scared, and I didn't blame him. It was frightening.

"Blue?" I looked at him. He could see me, and I could hear him.

"Can you hear me?" I asked. He nodded.

"What is this place?" he asked.

He was distressed, but he had no idea what this place was, and I wasn't thrilled about telling him.

"This is Limbus," I said. I watched for his reaction. It took a moment for it to sink in.

"Am I dead?" he asked. "Are you?"

"I don't think so," I said. "I think this is a place between life and death. I don't think we are dead yet." I explained.

"You don't think? How is that reassuring?" he said, unnerved.

"I wasn't trying to be reassuring."

Aspen didn't look too thrilled, and I wasn't his favourite person at the moment. He began to look around. The atmosphere was quite interesting to see if you hadn't seen it before, but after having been here for at least a few hours, I was beginning to feel crazy.

"Why isn't anybody moving?" Aspen asked.

"Well, I found that it was very exhausting moving when I had arrived. I don't know how you feel, but I can barely move. If these people have been here for a long while, I suspect that they lack any energy."

I watched as Aspen tried to move his legs, and I could tell by his stiff movements that he was struggling, just as I had.

"I guess you are right," he said, almost bitterly. I found it hard to stifle a smile. "Willow isn't here is she?" he asked.

"I hope not," I said. "I haven't seen her."

Aspens face visibly relaxed and I knew deep down that he and Willow would be alright.

I sat down, and Aspen followed suit. "How do we get out of here?"

"I have no idea."

We both fell silent as the negativity seemed to intensify. I was about to ask Aspen how he had got here when he solidified in front of me.

"NO!" I screamed.

CHAPTER FIFTY-EIGHT
WILLOW

"She was just a young girl," I screamed as Hazel laughed at my terror. Olive was slumped in a heap on the floor and there was nothing I could do to help her. She was gone.

"It was necessary," Hazel answered.

"How was that necessary?" I screamed once more. Hazel looked dumbstruck as if I was asking the most ridiculous questions.

"I was ageing, dear."

Suddenly, without me even realising, Hazel was gone in a whirl of darkness and I was left with this little girl who was so vulnerable. My heart ached for her and I couldn't stop the tears from falling. I readied myself to burn her, the ritual she so desperately deserved. However, when I called upon my abilities, they were gone. An emptiness inside me that I was only just discovering.

I picked Olive up, her body a dead weight in my arms and carried her to her parents' house.

I was not prepared for the scream that erupted when the door opened.

***

Walking home in a daze, I made a mental note to call a meeting. They had to know what had happened.

Sensing him behind me, I turned to find Aviv staring at me. He was too far away for me to notice the look on his face, however, his posture showed that he was on the defensive.

"What's wrong?" I asked. At the sound of my voice, Aviv began to move closer.

"I was hoping you could tell me," he answered.

"What do you mean?" I answered although I had a sinking feeling that I already knew the answer.

"My abilities aren't working," he said. I could hear a hint of fear in his voice.

"I know," I answered. "The ripple between Sationem and the human realm has diminished."

"Can it be fixed?" he almost whispered.

"If it can, I don't know how." I took a deep breath. "Blue isn't answering any of my calls right now and with the elemental magic gone, I cannot contact him, so I need you to help Poppy, okay?"

"I need to help Poppy do what?"

"To keep the Ventus community calm. They will listen to you." I turned around and began to walk away when a hand gripped my shoulder forcing me to stop.

"How am I supposed to keep them calm? Do you even realise the magnitude of what has happened?" Aviv asked.

"Of course, I do," I yelled, a little too harshly. "There is nothing that I can do until I have figured it out. Please. Just do as I ask."

I pulled myself away from him and watched his arm fall to the side before I stalked away. This time, Aviv did not follow.

CHAPTER FIFTY-NINE
WILLOW

"Bring it on," I whispered to myself as I looked over the horizon. The usual warm reds, oranges and golds of the sunrise had been replaced by the blackest of clouds.

Ignis had rarely seen rainfall in all the years since Sationem had been created, but it looked as if a storm were brewing; an unwelcome side effect of the ripple disappearing. The human realm was beginning to seep through.

I looked to the right and saw that the Youngers were starting to vacate their houses for the day. I hadn't yet told them of the disappearance of the abilities.

I took a deep breath and readied myself for the impact the news would bring to them. I stepped outside, the Youngers were talking amongst themselves. A few were watching the sky, their eyes widened. Ash noticed me as I was approaching.

"Willow," he said as he walked over. "What is happening?" he asked, gesturing towards the clouds that were now moving remarkably fast through the sky.

"Can everybody gather around please," I called out. They all very quickly moved forward, the murmuring amongst them becoming louder. I waited for it to stop.

"What's happening?" Ash repeated.

"Yeah, what's wrong with the sky?" Linden asked. Everybody looked upwards, some only just realising what all the fuss was about.

"The ripple, the barrier as some of you call it, between Sationem and the human realm is gone," I explained.

Acacia gasped. "What does that mean for Sationem?"

"I don't know," I answered. "For now, we will just leave the worrying to me and we will carry on as normally as possible." Everybody nodded in agreement, but the worry in their eyes was apparent.

"Let's get to training then," Acacia said. "Where's Olive?" she asked, looking around.

"There will be no training for the foreseeable future," I said, aware that this was the news I was most dreading to share. "Theory practice only," I added.

"Why?" Ash asked.

"When the ripple disappeared, so did our abilities."

"What?!" Ash and Linden shouted together. The uproar was exactly what I had expected.

"Calm down," I said. "I have a Tree Council meeting tomorrow and hopefully, I will find out what is happening." I looked around and I was pleased to see that they looked like they seemed to accept what I had said.

"I should go and tell Olive," Acacia said, slowly backing away from the group.

"Wait." I took a deep breath, not realising how difficult it was to say what was about to come out of my mouth.

"Willow?"

"I am afraid that Olive is no longer with us," I said.

"What do you mean?" Acacia asked.

"She died last night. I'm so sorry."

Acacia gasped, her hand flying to her mouth. "How?" she whispered.

"I cannot tell you much," I said. "Olive was in the wrong place at the wrong time."

"That's it?" Ash said. "That's all you're going to say?"

I nodded and watched as a few of them looked over at Linden. He was quiet when I revealed the news. Losing his sister was heart-breaking.

"At the moment, all I can say is be careful. Don't go out on your own. Stick together. Do not venture into the forest and do not approach anybody that you do not know." I looked around at them all. "Do you understand" There were a few murmurs and nodding of heads.

"Was it quick?" Acacia asked quietly.

I looked at her thinking of all that she had been through. "It was." I gave her a small smile. "Olive was a unique little girl and we will remember her fondly." I looked around at the group, their eyes glistening, looking younger and more vulnerable than ever. "I will let you know what happens tomorrow."

"Why didn't you say anything?" Ash asked Linden.

Linden shrugged. "I didn't want to think about it anymore. I was just hoping that we could get on with the training and forget about everything for a while." Linden explained. Acacia walked over to him and put her arms around him. Embracing him.

I left them all standing there as I turned and walked back to the house. It wasn't until I was safely inside that I let myself take a breath. The news I had just given had left me shaking.

CHAPTER SIXTY
WILLOW

When I arrived at Crownfire, the other Tree Leaders were already in position, and I could hear the raised voices from down on the ground.

Quickly, I positioned myself on my platform and readied myself for the assent. When the platform finally clicked into place above the flames, the other Tree Leaders fell silent.

"Nice of you to join us Willow," Oakley said, the sarcasm only barely noticeable.

"I thought I was early actually," I said to defend myself. "Since I was the one that called the meeting, don't you think that it is rather rude that you started without me?" I asked him, cocking my head.

"No, or we would have waited." Oakley drawled. "You are hardly in any position to call meetings girl, you are barely Awakened."

"Neither are you since you are only Glacies Second after all." The flames around me burned black and Oakley's face was turning redder and redder.

I looked around at the others. When my eyes rested on Poppy there was a questioning look in her eyes and I knew exactly what she was referring to. Blue wasn't there, and I still hadn't heard from him.

I shrugged my shoulders to answer her unasked question without raising difficult questions from the other Leaders.

"Willow," Dune began. "I know that you called this meeting, but currently, we have rather pressing concerns to deal with."

"I understand," I answered. "Is every Zone having the same problems with their abilities?" I asked.

"It seems so," Dune answered.

"What is causing it?" I asked.

"The ripple, as I understand it, is a very old magic that is controlled by the elements. The same elements that let our abilities work. When the ripple dissipated, the darkness spread." He explained.

"Darkness?"

"It could only be the work of dark magic that could make the ripple fall."

"Do you think this has something to do with Hazel?" I asked.

"Not this again," Oakley said, his voice a snarl.

"Why would you think that?" Lily asked, ignoring Oakley.

"The reason that I called this meeting," I said. "The night before it all happened, Hazel showed up in Ignis and killed a young girl. Olive."

"What did Olive do?" Lily asked, aghast.

"Nothing. Hazel simply said that she was ageing and needed Olive's soul to slow it down. Soon after, she teleported. I haven't seen her since."

"It is getting worse, Dune. Something needs to be done." Poppy said, unaware that she was drawing too much attention to the fact that Blue wasn't there.

"Where is your brother, Poppy?" Oakley asked. "Didn't he want to participate this morning?" Poppy looked over at me.

"I don't know where he is," she said quietly.

"What do you mean?" Dune asked.

"I haven't seen him for two days."

Everybody went quiet. The communities were dropping like flies and nobody seemed to know anything.

"Crimson have you found anything out yet?" Dune asked.

Shyly, Crimson appeared from behind her husband. "Not really, people are too scared to talk," she explained.

"You shouldn't be asking her to do this anyway, Dune. Anybody can see that it brings back harsh memories." Oakley said, for once sounding like he cared about his wife. The way he said it though, it sounded more like he wanted to rip somebodies throat out.

"Oakley, may I remind you that you are supposed to be suspended," Dune answered.

"Then why did you let me attend?" he asked, a smug smile on his face.

"I let you attend because, under these extremely strange and scary circumstances, we need all-hands-on-deck, and that includes yours." Oakley didn't say anything. "It might be helpful if you were to help Crimson with her task. You are unusually gifted at getting people to talk." Oakley simply nodded.

"What do we do about Hazel?" I asked.

"We will see what Oakley and Crimson can find out. We will convene in two days, at dawn. Hopefully Blue will have resurfaced by then too." He nodded to Poppy. "May I also ask where your brother is Willow?"

"I haven't seen him either," I said.

"Interesting," Dune said, and that was that. "Dismissed."

***

As I dragged myself out of bed, it seemed to take more energy than it usually did. In the mirror, it wasn't my face that looked back at me. The girl in the mirror was older, more gaunt-looking with shadows circling her eyes. Her skin was a sickly grey colour and even the colour of her eyes had dulled.

I sighed as I turned away from my reflection. I went to the window and peered out. I knew I shouldn't have gone to lay down after the meeting. I was so exhausted that I had slept for the rest of the day. The sky was still a mass of black clouds with no hint of the blue sky showing. It made Ignis dark and dreary, and the moods of the community seemed to reflect the weather.

As I turned away something caught my attention. It was quick, but it was there. I was sure of it.

I looked again, harder, scanning the trees. Scouring for a few more moments, squinting to see through the tree branches.

As I turned around to go to the kitchen I had to stifle a scream as I involuntarily jumped backwards.

"Blue?" I gasped. I stared at the form in front of me. It was Blue, and yet it wasn't. He was more ghost-like than a person. Transparent just like the souls I had seen in Limbus.

It suddenly occurred to me that this was Blue's soul.

"Blue, can you hear me?" I asked, but his transparent form just stood there. He seemed unable to communicate, and a few seconds later, he vanished.

"Blue?" I called and waited, but he didn't appear again.

CHAPTER SIXTY-ONE
WILLOW

I was back at Hazels resting place. After seeing Blue's soul, I knew, in my heart, that there was something wrong. As soon as I arrived, I knew for sure. I could feel them both.

"They are here, aren't they?" I asked. Hazel just smiled from the corner from where she watched me. "Show me where they are," I demanded.

"Very well."

Hazel took my arm and that unfamiliar turn of darkness appeared as she teleported us back down to the cave. I staggered as we landed and found myself in the very chamber that my mother died. Her bones were still there. Forrest's body was still there too, although burned now.

I turned towards the exit of the chamber and crossed over the threshold into the corridor beyond. I gasped as I saw what was in front of me.

The bodies of Blue and Aspen were lying side by side.

Soulless.

"They are not dead," Hazel said. "Yet."

"Bring them back," I demanded.

"Not until you agree to work with me. We could be very powerful together, you and I. I need you, and you need me," she said.

"I don't need you." I spat at her.

"You certainly do. There is nobody in your precious Tree Council that has experience in the type of abilities that you possess. There is nobody in any Zone with that kind of power. How do you expect to control it if there is no one to teach you how?" she said. "You need me."

I pondered what she had said for a moment. "I can learn to control these abilities myself. I am doing alright so far. What is to say that I wouldn't be fine?"

"You can take that chance, but what if something does happen. Something that you don't intend. What will you do then? You can't take it back."

"I will cross that bridge when it comes to it," I said.

Suddenly, Aspen's body erupted into flames.

"NO!" I shouted. "Stop it."

Aspens body burned on and I was helpless. I couldn't stop the flames, no matter how much I tried. I tried to conjure water or ice, but my abilities were not working.

"They won't work down here, or anywhere for that matter. Not until the ripple has been repaired." Hazel confirmed. "This is my lair; my power resides here. Only mine," she said laughing.

I was on my knees, crying. Blue's body was close to Aspen's and I moved him out of the way. Aspen was only bone and ash surrounded where his body once was. I couldn't breathe.

"Why did you do that?" I screamed. "He was all I had left."

"Oh, don't be so dramatic. You still have your father and your boy there," she said, indicating Blue's body.

"I don't though, do I? They aren't here. They are soulless, in Limbus." I screamed. Hazel clicked her fingers. Both my father and Blue appeared in transparent form. Neither of them could hear me. I didn't know if they could see me.

"I'll get both of you out, I promise," I said. "I will figure out a way." I had hardly finished my last word when they both disappeared.

CHAPTER SIXTY-TWO
HAZEL

I watched my daughter as the pain bled from her body. It was cruel, yes, killing her brother, but I had no choice. She had to be free of any distractions if she was to help me. Yes. It was the right thing to do.

"Bring him back," she pleaded, as her father and boy disappeared before her eyes. She was begging me. She was on her knees. I had a little sympathy, yes, but the long-term plan was more important than emotions.

"Once they are dead, they are gone. I cannot bring them back and neither can you." I explained. "However, I can teach you to bring back your father and Blue, but it will take time."

"How much time?" she asked. "Teach me, please."

"We cannot do it alone," I said. "We need another that is like us. We need the power of family."

She looked at me curiously. "How are we going to do that?" she asked.

"With my other insurance policy. I had to be sure that there was a second chance if you didn't work out."

"What do you mean?" she asked curiously.

"You have a brother. My son."

THE END

Printed in Great Britain
by Amazon